Woman In The Woods

Woman In The Woods

Phillip Tomasso

Other Books by Phillip Tomasso

NOVELS
Absolute Zero
Blood River
Preservation
Evacuation
Vaccination
Pigeon Drop
Convicted
Pulse of Evil
The Molech Prophecy (written as Thomas Philips)
Adverse Impact
Johnny Blade
Third Ring
Tenth House
Mind Play
You Choose

YOUNG ADULT NOVELS
Assassin's Promise
Queens of Osiris
Wizard's War
Wizard's Rise
Damn the Dead
Young Blood: The Nightbreed
Sounds of Silence

NOVELLAS
Extinction (A Novella)
Treasure Island: A Zombie Novella

FOR CHILDREN
Jay Walker: Case of the Impractical Prankster
Jay Walker: Case of the Missing Action Figure

This book is for Jenny.
If you know me
You know who Jenny is.
If you know who Jenny is
You know why this book
Is for her…

Chapter 1

Elissa Crosby tossed and turned, troubled by a nagging suspicion something wasn't right. The knock at the front door gave her a reason to get out of bed. She lit the lantern on the nightstand and pulled on her robe. The waning light flickered as she crossed the parlor and she stopped when the sinking feeling in her stomach weighted down her legs and feet.

The knock came again.

A shadow backlit by moonlight darkened the curtained glass on the door. Her lips quivered and while the idea of going back to bed, getting under the covers and finding sleep became appealing, she forced herself forward. "Just a minute."

There were few times when Elissa missed having a husband. When the roof leaked and the lonely bed on a winter night was cold were two. The man she'd unfortunately married was a bastard. Quick-tempered and violent, getting rid of him was one of the smartest things she'd ever done in her life. Although the bruises were gone and the broken bones had healed, the scars no one saw would last a lifetime. It was a shame she'd wasted ten years hiding before wizening up. However, she'd feel more comfortable having a man answer the door in the middle of the night. That would be a third thing she missed. There was no man and just like everything else, she was the one responsible for getting things done.

She unlocked and opened the door. A brisk breeze brought to life the sea glass and driftwood wind chimes before rushing past her. She shivered and hugged her robe tightly against the cold temperature as dead, brown leaves rustled across the high grass out front.

The sheriff stood on her front step with his Stetson in his hands in front of his chest. He spun the hat by the brim. "Hate to bother you at this time of night, Elissa."

Small towns. First names. Benji O'Sullivan was about her age, maybe a year or two older. Relief filled her for just a moment. O'Sullivan at the door was better than some stranger, but it made her wonder. Why was he here, at her door, in the middle of the night? "Is everything alright, sheriff?"

"Mind if I come in?"

She stepped aside. "Not at all, but I don't mind telling you, I'm feeling rather apprehensive about a late night visit."

What happened to calling me Elissa? "Ma'am, Ms. Crosby, we've found a body. Is your daughter home?"

"At this hour, she's asleep in her room … if the knocking didn't wake her, that is."

"Could you check?"

"Sheriff?" Elissa put an arm across her waist, hoping she could stop the flip flopping. It didn't help. "I am certain she didn't witness any foul play. I am certain of it."

The sinking feeling she had the last few hours, the reason she couldn't sleep—her legs wouldn't respond; she was glued in place.

"Elissa?"

"Can you tell me what this is about? Alice has to be up early in the morning. I'd rather not disturb her if I don't have to. Perhaps there is a question I can answer for you?" She bit down on her lower lip and only let up when she feared she'd draw blood.

"We recovered a body in the hills not far from here."

"My Alice wouldn't know anything about that." Elissa rolled the hand across her belly into a tight fist. Sharp fingernails dug into her palms.

"I wasn't sure, but I thought she looked a lot like your Alice."

Elissa shook her head. "No, that's not possible. She's here. In her room. In bed."

"When was the last time you checked on her?"

When was the last time she'd checked on Alice? "She wasn't feeling well, barely ate her supper and asked to be excused."

The sheriff's eye twitched. "When was supper?"

His features were cast in an eerie mix of candlelight and shadow. Elissa didn't care for the way the man looked when the flame danced or the way dark and light played over his eyes. "Around about five-thirty, six."

The sheriff pulled out a pocket watch. "It's nearly three in the morning now."

She didn't appreciate the implication. "My daughter was sick, sheriff. She went to bed early."

"I am not doubting you, ma'am." He held up both hands as if pacifying her. Instead she felt patronized. "I'd be remiss if we didn't at least look in on her. I hope I'm wrong ma'am, that I disturbed your night for no reason. If she's under those covers asleep, I'm satisfied. There'll be no need to wake her."

She ignored the beads of sweat dotting her forehead; more perspiration pooled behind her knees and inside her clenched fist. She kept looking toward the back of the house, where the bedrooms were. "I don't know what good it will do."

"It will give me peace of mind, ma'am."

She wished he would go back to using her first name. It sounded more official and troubling when he was formal.

"Ma'am?"

"Oh, alright. You just wait here. I'll check. I'm sorry it is going to be a little dark. I only have the one lamp."

"I'll be fine."

She pursed her lips, not caring if the sheriff saw her look of discontent. Elissa shuffled down the hall, past her own room and hesitated with her hand over the knob of her daughter's door. She stopped, unable to move. Fear and panic set in. Her stomach didn't just ache, instead everything inside of her sizzled with anxiety. "Sheriff? Can you come here, please."

He would have to maneuver through the dark. Elissa didn't turn around when she heard his footsteps behind her.

"I can't open the door."

"It's locked?" he asked.

"No." She shook her head. This was the reason she'd been unable to sleep. She hadn't known it at the time but now understood the cause behind the trepidation she'd felt now. "I'm afraid."

The sheriff reached around, twisted the knob and pushed open the door.

Elissa handed over the lantern. She couldn't bring herself to look inside her daughter's room.

The dim light barely penetrated the darkness beyond the doorway.

Helplessly, Elissa forced herself to peer into the darkness. She didn't need sunlight to see Alice's bed was empty.

Dropping onto her knees, Elissa screamed. "No, no-no-no!"

Chapter 2

Rochester, NY — Present Day

"You're going home, Jeremy." The nurse offered up a warm smile. Dressed in hospital blues, hair pulled back, she set a tentative hand on his arm.

Jeremy almost shied away from the contact, but refrained. It went against every instinct. Fighting those urges helped convince doctors he was better. Instead, he folded the last t-shirt from his dresser drawer and placed it on the bed next to his other belongings.

"Are you excited?"

He nodded. Excited was not the word. Afraid worked better. All he'd known the last nine years were the white halls of St. Mary's. Maybe he shouldn't have concentrated so much effort on convincing doctors of anything. He wouldn't be here now, packing his things. It was movie night. He could be microwaving a bag of popcorn and picking out a recliner in the rec room in anticipation of the flick. It didn't matter what was showing. Movie night was best.

"A little scared?" she asked.

He nodded. "A little."

"That's okay."

She'd faltered, as if she were going to say, *that's normal*, but stopped herself in time.

"You'll be staying with your uncle?"

He wished the conversation would end. There was nothing comfortable about it. Sure, the questions came across as simple. Part of him felt as if he were still being tested, observed. "I was eight when they brought me here. I don't really remember him very well."

Although he was afraid to leave, he was also ready to go. The psychiatric floor he lived on housed people who terrified him at times. When Bobby wasn't standing in a corner talking to the walls, he was punching himself in the face hard enough that he'd broken his nose a time or two. CarryAnn ate anything she could get her hands on. Countless nights she was transported to Strong so the E.R. doctors could pump her stomach. Jethro hated wearing clothing. Orderlies never had it easy when after chasing him up and down halls, they were forced to tackle and restrain the large naked and violent man.

"He's visited with you many times."

Visits were awkward. He and Uncle Jack sat at a table in the rec room and talked about the weather, or a football, or baseball game, even though Jeremy cared less about sports than he did about weather. "Yes, he has."

There was nothing else to fold. Everything he owned was stacked neatly on the bed. He should turn and face the nurse, but couldn't bring himself to do it. Keeping his arms at his side, he stared at his things and patiently waited for her to give up on trying and just leave.

And eventually, when the silence dragged on, she left.

* * *

Dr. Brian Burkhart sat at his desk. Books filled tall cases behind him. Leaning back in his chair, his elbows on the rests, he tapped fingertips together in a pyramid below his chin. His grey hair was neatly parted down the middle and his soft blue dress shirt freshly pressed. A white lab coat hung on a rack in the corner nearest the wall displaying an array of framed degrees. Regarding his visitors over the rim of thick lens eye glasses, he smiled. "Mr. Raines, it is good to see you this morning."

"You, as well, doctor."

Jack, a large man, sat straight in an uncomfortable wood chair with broad shoulders back and beefy arms resting on the armrests. He kept hands folded together in his lap. With a full head of deer-brown hair, wide-set eyes and a strong chin, Jeremy wondered if this were a glimpse into what he'd look like in his forties.

"And how are you today, Jeremy?"

Innocuous as the question sounded, answering became a bit more complex. Taking too much time could be perceived as awkward and calculated.

"I'm well. Thank you."

It seemed unwise pointing out his stomach was unsettled. He wasn't sure if he needed to move his bowels or vomit. On the verge of perspiring, Jeremy kept his breathing even, calm. Conflicted, he was afraid of going home, but he didn't want to spend another night inside the institution. Freedom scared him. Staying at the hospital would drive him insane. That is, if he wasn't already out of his mind.

"Since Jeremy earned his G.E.D. while a resident here, I understand, Mr. Raines, you've secured work for your nephew?" Dr. Burkart kept arms on the desk, fingers interlaced in front of him. He leaned forward, his interest apparent and seemingly genuine.

Jack used a fist to cover his mouth when he cleared his throat. "Yes, sir. Nothing fancy really. Diner in town. He'll be working in back. It's one of the only places to eat, so it's a busy spot."

"That's splendid. My first job was as a busboy for a party house. Long, long hours, but it taught me about work ethic." Dr. Burkart nodded, silently, as if finishing his thought silently.

Jeremy tried paying attention. Instead, he studied his Uncle Jack's profile. Clean shaven, with wrinkles at the corner of his eyes. *He looks like my father*, Jeremy thought.

Dr. Burkhart said, "Jeremy?"

"Yes. A busboy sounds like a challenging job."

"Well. I'm not sure how challenging it was. The point is, I learned plenty from working there. Overall, it was an experience.

I've been thankful for the opportunity from my first day employed."
Dr. Burkhart smiled, his eyes bright, hopeful.

Must be nice. Always optimistic and positive.

"My first job was mowing lawns in the summer and shoveling drive-ways in the winter." Uncle Jack returned the smile, a stiff expression. "Made a lot of money, but I broke my back."

The conversation had turned somewhat surreal and Jeremy handled it best by just smiling and nodding. He wanted out of the small office. He'd have sworn the walls moved. Could the room have been shrink-ing? He took in a slow, deep breath. He felt the perspiration pool in the recess of his throat and collarbone. It was definitely getting hotter. Jeremy tugged at his t-shirt, but stopped and dropped his hand into his lap. He didn't want anything he did perceived as mental illness.

If they revoked his release, he might scream; he would scream.

Screaming didn't sound extreme.

Maybe he was healed and deserved to go home?

He shook his head. If he were better, then why was the office getting smaller and hotter? No one else seemed to notice. Uncle Jack didn't look uncomfortable, or worried.

"Is everything alright?" Dr. Burkhart asked.

"I've never had a job before."

Uncle Jack shifted his weight around. He faced his nephew. "It's not much different than going to school. You get up every morning and go to work. Think of your boss like a teacher, or something. You do what they say. Only instead of getting homework, you get a paycheck."

Jeremy hated school. Bullies made the experience hell. He'd been in more fights than he could remember. Usually, he was on the losing side. Countless black eyes, fat lips and bloody noses still plagued many of his dreams. It was never one-on-one either. He recalled attempts at defending himself against groups of boys. "A paycheck sounds good," he said and offered up a smile.

The taunting. That was almost always worse than the beatings. The name calling and knocking books out of his hands bothered him more than getting shoved or punched in the back.

The idea of work being anything like school made him apprehensive.

Maybe he'd been wrong about wanting out of St. Mary's. If anything, living behind these padded walls had been safe.

Was there a right thing to want?

Should he talk about this more with Dr. Burkhart?

"I have a question." Jeremy froze. He'd surprised himself by speaking.

Dr. Burkhart leaned forward. Genuine interest filled his expression as his eyes widened in anticipation. "Yes,. Jeremy?"

"If I want to come back, may I?"

Jeremy wasn't sure what he expected. When the doctor sat back in his chair and grinned, he knew that was the opposite reaction anticipated.

"You're going to be just fine, son. If we didn't believe you were ready to go home with your uncle, then we wouldn't be here right now. You asking that question tells me the board has made the right decision. The years spent here have helped you tremendously. You've come a long way. The only way you're going to grow as a person now is by getting back out into the world. I know it can seem frightening. There are many, many new things you'll experience and that you should experience. But inside that folder is my card and if you ever feel the need to talk, about anything, you can call me. Night or day, Jeremy. Do you understand? I will still be here for you. In fact, my feelings will be hurt if you don't call every once in a while just to let me know how you're doing. How does that sound?"

It still sounded scary. "Thank you, Dr. Burkhart."

"You don't have to thank me. Just make sure you call. Do I have your word?" Dr. Burkhart stood up.

Jack got to his feet.

Jeremy, not wanting to be the only one still sitting, stood up as well. "You have my word."

Chapter 3

Jeremy placed his guitar case and bags in the back of Jack's truck. He climbed into the cab and fastened his seatbelt, doing his best to ignore the knot tightening inside around his gut. It wasn't until after they pulled out of the St. Mary's parking garage that he sensed some relief and allowed himself a small sigh. They were headed home. He wasn't positive how he felt about the move yet, but he knew he was at least ready for change.

Jack's air conditioner hummed, blowing icy air out from corner vents. Jeremy didn't mind. Although Labor Day was on Monday, the month of August had already taken its toll. It had been both a hot and terribly humid summer and he didn't like sweating. The hospital A/C was never strong enough to cool down the ward, or more specifically, *his* room.

"Is it too cold? You can adjust it however you want." His fingers fidgeted with the settings on the dash controls. The air died.

Jeremy shook his head. "No. I like it."

Jack switched it back on and pulled his hand away. "You sure?"

"Yeah. It feels good." Jeremy readjusted the seatbelt across his chest. The nylon cut into the side of his neck, made his skin red and itchy. He couldn't recall ever having ridden in the front seat of a vehicle before. Even when the ward went on day trips, they took a van. If there was room, he sat in back.

The sun, painfully bright in a cloudless, blue sky, caused a brilliant white glare off of the windshield. Jeremy raised a hand and shielded his eyes.

"You can lower the visor, if you want." Jack pointed.

Jeremy looked up at the edge of papers peeking out. He didn't want to make a mess. Squinting against sunlight was fine, no big deal. "I'm good."

Jack reached over and snatched the items secured above the visor, turned them over in his hand and then handed them to Jeremy. "Stuff those in the glove box for me?"

The glove box was already crammed. "Not sure it will fit."

"Stuff it right in. Slam it closed." He laughed when Jeremy struggled keeping papers from jetting out before the box latched closed. After several attempts, he was successful. "There you go."

Jeremy inadvertently rolled his eyes, caught himself and hoped his uncle missed it. He wasn't being ungrateful as much as he felt embarrassed about struggling with something as simple as a glove box.

"Want some music? We have about a four hour drive ahead of us."

Making small talk took a lot of work. Even though Jeremy appreciated his uncle taking him in, there was no polite way of saying he'd be fine if they drove the entire way in complete silence. The hospital was so full of constant noises; someone yelling, or crying, or talking.

Would he still have been released if he had no home to return to? If his Uncle Jack hadn't agreed to take him in? He'd never asked anyone that question before. It didn't seem important at the time. Now, he found himself a little curious. "Music would be great," Jeremy said.

"Okay." Jack nodded with such enthusiasm it was as if the two of them had agreed on doing something crazy and bonding and full of significance, instead of turning on the radio. Loud music came from the speakers. "I'm not sure what you like. You can put on whatever station you want."

Jeremy shrugged. St. Mary's piped instrumental stuff through speakers most of the day. Although the songs played softly in the background, *it* was always there and—playing day-in and day-out—usually gave him something of a headache. "Whatever you like is fine, really."

He wanted to be polite and prove taking him in hadn't been a mistake.

Jack let out a long sigh, unrolled his fingers and re-gripped the steering wheel. "Can I say something?"

Jeremy's throat went dry. Afraid his voice might crack if he spoke, he nodded.

"I want to be honest, okay? Straight forward? I'm real nervous about this. Real nervous. Your father, he was my only brother. You're my last kin. We're family. I know you needed your time away, time to get better and everything. But those people at the hospital didn't just give you to me." Jack turned and pointed at his nephew. "I fought for you. I wanted you home."

"You did?"

"Yeah." Jack focused on the road. He shifted his weight in his seat. "Thing is, what do I know about kids?" He rolled a hand around near his head. "I have all these memories of my mother, your grandmother—she passed before you were born—and I just remember the things she did for me and your father. She was the best woman, I swear. No one could ask for a better mother."

Jeremy's eyes twitched and he looked away.

"I'm sorry," Jack said. "I wasn't thinking. See, but that's my point. What I'm trying to say is I have no idea what to say, or do. I don't even know how to act."

"You're doing fine. I'm uncomfortable, too. I don't want to do anything wrong." Jeremy left the rest of his thought unspoken, *he didn't want his uncle sending him back to St. Mary's.* He'd been free of the institution less than a half hour and already he was less apprehensive about going home.

He felt admittedly hopeful.

"Well, okay. Good, then. We're on the same page here. So let's both just relax. We give it some time, get used to having each other around, get used to when to stay out of each other's way and such and I think this will work out fine. *Whadya* say?"

It sounded perfect. "Deal."

Jack held out his hand, eyes still on the road. "Put 'er there."

They shook.

"Okay. Put on some music and let's enjoy the ride home."

Jeremy reached for the radio knob. "It's okay, you know."

Jack said, "What is?"

Missing his mother and father, loss was one thing Jeremy spent years working on. It was the crux of his one-on-one therapy and often came up during Dr. Burkhart's group sessions. Accepting that their deaths weren't his fault was quintessential to recovery. Overcoming sleepless nights and an endless plague of nightmares when he could sleep, Jeremy found new ways of coping with life. "I'm sure my grandmother was a great woman. I wish I could have met her."

At this, Jack grinned. "You'd have loved her and she'd have spoiled you rotten."

Chapter 4

Fort Keeps, NY — Adirondacks

"Does any of it look familiar?" Jack smiled.

Jeremy didn't think he'd recognize a thing, that he'd been gone far too long to remember. He felt a comfortable squeeze as they crept through the mountains. It was almost as if the mountains were a protective entity but could easily have been mistaken as foreboding or constricting. Tall leafy trees lining either side of the road softened some of the phobia.

Through breaks in the trees was nothing but placid water. They were almost home. Jeremy pointed out the window. "Fourth Lake?"

"That's right."

He felt like a child again. In a good way. In what he perceived was a normal way. He found he was breathing more evenly. The knot he'd had earlier in his gut suddenly splintered apart and faded away.

Home.

It suddenly felt like more than just a word or some topic discussed in group. He couldn't hide his smirk. Staring out the window, he watched the boats on the water and people swimming closer to the banks.

Jack turned off the main road andpicked up speed. There were no posted limit signs. While the road was still paved, it was more pitted and cracked. The ride transitioned from smooth to bumpy. The foliage became denser, big branches rose up and crossed over like a canopy, casting down a blanket of shadows.

Jeremy knew Dr. Burkhart had given his uncle his prescriptions. He wasn't sure why he thought about them now. His palms itched. It was a sign of anxiety for him. He wouldn't need more of anything until before bed.

"Did you live near us?" Jeremy remembered his house, only he saw it more in snapshots passing through his memories. Cracked front steps led up to a split-level house with flat grey clapboard, where most of the paint curled up off the wood. He remembered Dad left cans of paint, an aluminum extension ladder and a paint spattered tarp on the front lawn. Mom always said every few years the whole place needed a fresh coat, the clapboard just drank up the paint.

Jeremy had no idea what that meant. All he knew was that it had been the summer his father was going to let him help. He couldn't wait. Climbing the ladder and painting a house. The time with his dad was going to be the best.

Then they were murdered.

And he went away.

"So what do you think about that?" Jack said, eyebrows raised and clearly anticipating an upbeat response.

Jeremy, however, hadn't been listening. It happened at times, too often, actually. His mind pulled him off in different directions. Getting back wasn't always easy. Some of the St. Mary nurses insisted on using physical contact to regain his attention; a hand on his shoulder, a finger on his arm. "Sounds good," Jeremy answered, knowing something needed to be said.

"Wonderful. That's wonderful."

The road wound through the trees. The mountains rose again on either side. The small town of Fort Keeps couldn't be much further. Jeremy thought the hours had passed by quickly, especially after they'd entered the Adirondack region.

"Got Big Moose Lake on the left." Jack indicated with his elbow.

Jeremy didn't see a lake. He saw the crag of the mountains, trunks of tall trees and leaves. He knew of Big Moose, though. He couldn't recall ever having visited. Fort Keeps had the Chahta Lake and behind his old house was Pigeon Creek, which in the spring ran like a river and fed into most of the lakes in the area.

Jeremy didn't recognize the sign post. *Welcome to Fort Keeps* was carved into the wood and *Welcome* was imposed on an oblong green marque. The Fort Keeps letters were raised. Carved in around the words for atmosphere were pine trees and brown bears.

And then, Jeremy was home.

"Uncle Jack?" Jeremy shifted his weight around and faced his uncle. "Where do you live?"

Jack laughed, but it came out something more like a grunt. "What? Are you joking?"

Shaking his head, Jeremy shrugged. "I, ah, I don't think so."

"We just talked about it."

There was one street light at the four-way intersection. Main Street had a few small businesses.

When I wasn't listening, he thought. "Well yeah, I know. I just forgot."

"You weren't listening, were you?"

He thought about lying. "I wasn't. I'm sorry."

Jeremy recognized the look of the street and while some things had changed, a lot was exactly the same as he remembered.

There was a hardware store, diner, a one-screen movie theater, cafe, bakery, convenience store and gas station, a corner bar, pizza place, a liquor store, the sheriff's office, a post office, two-door fire department and a general supply store. The town divided naming things with either Fort Keeps, or Chahta at the beginning.

"That's where you're going to be working. Right there."

Jeremy didn't remember the names of all the locations. He was sure some had changed. However, the diner looked the same. "Danny's Diner?"

"Danny's Diner. And just at the end of the road, right over there? That's where I work. Lead Foot Auto Repairs."

"You fix cars?"

"All day long."

For the first time, Jeremy noticed grease lining his uncle's finger-nails. "I didn't mean for that to sound bad."

"I didn't take it that way. Hey, it's not a problem … about the house?" he asked, as they drove through town. Jack turned left at the light. The road immediately inclined and shifted into a lower gear.

Jeremy's mouth felt dry.

The town looked a little different. The nice carved sign was new to him. Not this road.

"I had been saying," Jack said, "your parents left everything to you in their will. It wasn't much. The house, some money in an account you can have at twenty-one and they named me as their executor. And that's just fancy legal jargon for having me handle the finances and stuff. I was between places and got court permission after showing them I could cut out hiring maintenance workers and such and save them money, well, you, by moving in."

"Moving in, where?" The knot was back in his gut.

"Your house," Jack said.

Snapshot flashed behind his eyeballs. He saw a bloodied kitchen counter. There was a red handprint on the half curtain over the small window above the sink.

"Been living there about six years now." Jack kept stealing glances at his nephew.

They pulled onto a long, dirt and gravel covered driveway. "You live here? *My* house?" Jeremy thought his body iced over. He couldn't move a limb, not even to blink.

Ahead, Jeremy saw atop a well-manicured patch of lawn, cement stairs. They were no longer cracked and a handrail had been installed on either side. The clapboard looked freshly painted. Leaning against the side of the house was his father's ladder and tarp.

Jeremy remembered the big tree in front. Jeremy's father made and hung a single rope swing with a plank for him to sit on. He'd push Jeremy for what seemed like hours at the time. He remembered his mother on the front porch, arms loosely folded, laughing as she watched. The tree was still there. The swing was gone.

"*Jer?* Jeremy? Are you okay?"

Chapter 5

The first thing Jeremy realized: he was still sitting inside his uncle's truck. The seat belt fabric irritated his neck. When his vision returned, it came in colorful swirls and he reached out his hand touching the dash for balance. Everything, slowly, came into focus. The passenger door was open. Uncle Jack stood beside him and was holding him by the shoulders.

"Uncle Jack?"

Jack couldn't hide his apprehension. With eyes open wide, concern forced his eyebrows together like a pyramid beneath creases across his forehead. "Are you okay?"

"I think I'm just tired." It was a blatant lie. Jeremy thought his uncle knew it too. Seemed easier than either admitting he'd fainted. He had no way of knowing how long he'd blacked out for without asking and he had no intention of asking. "This is just—leaving the hospital, coming home—it's a little overwhelming."

"Sure. I understand that." Jack took a step back. "I have your old room all ready for you. New sheets. New bedspread. I bought you some new jeans and t-shirts. But, hey, anything you don't like we'll just take back. Let you pick out what you want. That's what I should have done anyway. I didn't think that through. I just wanted everything all ready for you. How many kids want their uncle buying them back-to-school clothes? I'm sorry, Jer."

Jack had been sending him jeans and t-shirts at St. Mary's for the last several years. Jeremy said, "I'm sure everything's fine. I mean, you've been doing pretty good this long."

"Yeah?" Jack finally relaxed.

"No complaints."

"Okay." Jack nodded his head, appreciatively. "Let me help you get your things. I see you've still got the guitar. Been playing?"

"All the time." The guitar was his therapy. Even Dr. Burkhart admitted music was good for the soul. "Music is a moral law. It gives soul to the universe, wings to the mind, flight to the imagination and charm and gaiety to life and to everything."

"Who said that? You make that up?"

"Me? No. Dr. Burkhart said it all the time, only I think he was quoting Plato."

Jack said, "The dog?"

Jeremy laughed. "The philosopher."

"Just teasing."

"Hope so," Jeremy said, still laughing. He couldn't imagine not having it. Jack sent it to him as a Christmas gift the year before. "But seriously, that guitar—it's the best gift anyone's ever given me."

Only Jack sent him gifts on his birthday and for Christmas. It was like he'd said, they only had each other. They were it. They were family.

"Thought you'd like it. When I was your age I had a guitar like that."

"You still play?"

Jack took a rock star stance. His boots kicked up dust. "Nope. Learned a few chords. Played the beginnings of a few Eagles and Elvis songs and then the rest of the time I just daydreamed about making it big. Didn't know it then, but without practicing, without putting in the hard work, there's no record deals. No groupies. No world-wide tour. Let that be a lesson to ya."

Jeremy laughed. "Got it."

"Come on. Let's get inside out of the heat."

* * *

With a backpack over a shoulder and his guitar case in hand, Jeremy followed his uncle into the house. Jack stopped just inside. He lifted a ring of keys off a hook on the wall.

"These are for you," Jack said. "Was a time when no one in the mountains locked their doors. Crime's everywhere. One key does the lock and the dead bolt."

Jeremy turned the ring over in his hand. "There's three keys."

"One is for my truck. You don't drive it without permission. We understand each other?"

Jeremy cocked his head to one side. "I don't even know how to drive, so I don't think that will be an issue."

"Go throw your stuff in your room. Then we'll go outside. I want to show you what the third key is for."

Jeremy stood still for a moment, expecting an explanation. When none came, he moved through the front living room and up the stairs, avoiding the kitchen altogether.

His parents' bedroom was at the end of the hall on the left. Bathroom on the right. His room was the first door on the right and a spare across the hall.

Jack must have painted. Although he couldn't recall the previous color, the hallway was now a deep maroon, white trim. There was a small table in the center of the hall, an overlapping off-white doily laid under an antique lamp. Jeremy hit the switch at the top of the stairs. The bulb in the ceiling fixture came on. He walked over to the table. Switched the lamp on. Neither light was needed. He continued to his room with an eye on the closed door into his parents' bedroom. Before entering his room, he stepped back and looked into the spare. The bed was made, but there was clothing strewn about on the floor, as well as folded and stacked inside a laundry basket by the dresser.

Uncle Jack must use this room, he thought.

Jeremy pushed open his door. He expected memories to flood and was prepared for a sensory overload. It never came.

The walls, smelled recently painted, were lapis blue. There was a matching blue and black lined bedspread and matching drapes. A six drawer dresser was against a wall near the window and a horizontal six drawer dresser stood against the wall by the closet.

"Come on, Jeremy!"

Jeremy set his bag down on the bed and leaned the guitar case against the wall. He went to the window and looked out across the front yard. His Uncle Jack was in the grass looking back up and him, waving encouragingly for him to hurry it up.

Nodding, he backed away from the window and turned around.

Someone passed by his open bedroom door.

Startled, Jeremy backed into the wall.

He stood, waiting.

Waiting.

He didn't dare move, or make a sound. *Maybe Uncle Jack has a friend living here?*

He'd have mentioned it.

Wouldn't he have?

He tried moving. One step. He couldn't lift his foot off the floor. His hands went to his thigh. Jeremy thought he might have to physically move his leg. Staggering, he walked toward the door. Every creak in the floorboards made him stop and listen.

His heart pounded inside his chest as he worked up enough courage to look out into the hallway.

The lights went out.

He took another step back. There was no problem moving backwards. None.

His breath caught in his chest.

Someone filled the doorway. Big.

"Jeremy!"

Jeremy screamed.

"Whoa!" Jack had a hand across his chest. "I didn't mean to scare you."

Jeremy sat on the bed, panting. "Just wasn't expecting you. Thought you were outside."

"I was. I have been waiting like ten minutes."

Ten minutes? That wasn't possible. He'd been in his room only seconds. Two minutes tops. "I was just looking around."

"I get that. I appreciate that. But, as long as you're alright, come on." He looked excited, like he couldn't stand still in one place for long. "You alright?"

"I'm okay."

"Well, come on then!" He ran out of the room, still hollering for him to follow from down the stairs.

Jeremy looked both ways. No one was in the hallway. The door to his parents' room was opened, though.

He started that way.

When a shadow passed across the wall inside the room, Jeremy backed into the corner of the table. The lamp wobbled. He spun around and caught it after it fell, but before it had hit the floor.

The bedroom door slammed shut.

Jeremy twisted toward the sound.

The lamp cord wrapped around and toppled the table. He fell forward. The lamp smashed under him. The bulb popped. He saw a black dots cross in front of his eyes.

"Jer?" Jack bounded up the stairs. "What happened?"

"I tripped."

"Here. Let me help you." Jack took the crushed lamp. "Careful of the glass. I think, you know what? Why don't you take a nap? You said you were tired. I shouldn't have rushed you like that. I just got excited, you know? It was selfish."

Jeremy wanted to comfort his uncle. There were no words.

Maybe he was tired.

His palms itched. "I might need my meds."

"Ah, yeah," Jack said. "They're in the kitchen. Let me grab them. I'll get you some water."

Jack lifted Jeremy off the ground, helped him into the bedroom.

"I think I am going to lie down. Just for a bit."

"Absolutely, Jer. Tell you what? I'll make a nice early dinner and let you know when it's ready. Wait here. I'll get your medication. Be right back."

When Jack left the room, Jeremy pushed his back against the headboard. He raised his knees and wrapped his arms around his legs. He stared at the window.

His mind replayed the things he saw.

The things he thought he saw.

They were memories. Nothing more.

Memories didn't slam doors or cut power to lights.

He stopped thinking, closing his eyes tight. It was his imagination. Coming home stirred things inside him. That made the most sense. It was a viable explanation.

"I don't really know which ones you need." Jack held three pill bottles in 0ne hand and a glass of water with ice cubes in the other. He held each item as if they were fragile, he was even stooped forward like he thought he might trip and drop everything.

"Thank you." Jeremy took the bottles.

Jack set the water down on a coaster on the nightstand. "You okay?"

"I just need time. Coming back here, I guess it just wasn't something I expected."

"I'm sorry, Jer. Maybe it was something I should have discussed with Burkhart." Jack looked around. "I should maybe call him?"

Jeremy twisted open the clonazepam and poured a pill out onto his palm. "I'll be fine. Honestly."

Jack picked up the water, held it out to Jeremy. "You rest. Take as long as you need."

Jeremy dropped the pill into his mouth, sipped the water and replaced it on the nightstand. When Jack was at the door, Jeremy said, "Uncle Jack?"

He turned around.

"I'm sorry if I ruined today for you."

Jack came back into the room. He sat on the edge of the bed. "Let me tell you something. Having you home is the greatest thing. You haven't ruined a thing. Things are going to work out. I just need to remember that some adjustment time is needed. I get that now."

"Thanks, Uncle Jack."

"I'm happy to have you home." At the door, Jack stopped. "You want it open?"

Jeremy thought about the person who passed by his room moments ago. "Closed, please."

He shut the door, softly until the latch clicked.

Jeremy laid down, bunched up his pillow. He stared at the door.

Part of him expected the knob to turn.

He waited.

And waited.

Finally, he turned onto his right side and faced the window. He didn't realize he was crying until he felt his cheek touch the wet, cold pillow case.

He left the tears alone and closed his eyes.

Chapter 6

Jeremy opened his eyes. Darkness surrounded him. Everything had been a dream. All of it. He knew the smell. The air conditioner was on and antiseptic permeated the room.

St. Mary's?

He sat up, put a hand to his head, but it didn't stop the slow spin of the room. Dizzy, he stood up, reached out and touched a wall for balance.

It was wrong. He was wrong. This wasn't St. Mary's.

He bent toward the window. Lightning flashed.

In the glass reflection he saw his mother standing behind him. Blood covered half of her face. He turned to face her, his back against the window.

The room was pitch black. He couldn't see the bed he'd just climbed out of, until a second bolt of lightning lit the world behind him. His mother stood nose to nose. Her mouth wide open. Maggots spilled out as her tongue protruded and she screamed...

...Jeremy sprang up in bed. Eyes wide.

He was covered in a cold sweat, his shirt sticking to his skin. Clapping a hand over his heart, he took in his surroundings.

The blue walls. His guitar case leaned against wall.

Breathing short, shallow breaths he picked up the glass of water. The ice had melted. A wet ring was on the cork of the coaster. His hand trembled. Taking only a tentative sip, Jeremy did his best to control the panic attack he felt coming on.

It was a nightmare. Just a nightmare.

* * *

Jeremy slept for nearly two hours. There was nothing early about their dinner. When they finished eating, Jeremy cleared the table and put the plates in the sink. As he turned on the water, Jack said, "That can wait. Follow me."

Outside the sun had crossed most of the sky and was behind the tall trees west of the patch of property. Shadows blanketed the front yard and backyard, for that matter. Jack strode toward the driveway. He stopped in front of the garage door and faced his nephew. "Ready?"

"Sure?"

"You don't sound positive." Jack's jaw set and he rocked on the balls of his feet, fists on his sides. His expression lightened and he snickered. "I'm just joshing!"

Jeremy wasn't sure he caught the gist of the joke, but forced out a polite laugh. Barely.

Jack turned, squatted and raised the garage door. "Well? You like it? It's for you. It's yours."

Inside, the garage was packed full. White sheets were draped over furniture and stacked boxes. There were power tools on pegs on the wall and a tall red tool box in the corner. There was a riding lawn-mower, next to a push mower and in the center, as if on display, was the only possible gift Jeremy could see. "The motorcycle? That's mine?"

"Well. It's not a motorcycle. It's a scooter. Don't make that face. It goes up to ninety miles an hour. Not that you need that kind of speed around here. Tank of gas should last you a month. Come winter we'll have to think of something better, like a car. But I wasn't sure if you knew how to drive." Jack walked into the garage and lifted the simple black helmet off the seat.

Jeremy saw flashes. He sat on his father's lap inside a car. The windows down. Car tires crunched over loose gravel in a parking lot. He had the wheel, tight in both hands. Barely seeing over the hood of the car, his father encouraged him to spin the wheel this way and that. "I've never driven a car."

"Well this is easy." Jack climbed onto the scooter. "Twist this like so, to go. Press this to stop. It's really like riding a bike. Did you, do you know how to ride a bike?"

"I know how to ride a bike," Jeremy said.

"What do you say? Want to take it for a spin?"

"I kinda do, yeah." Jeremy didn't try hiding his smile.

"You better 'kinda' want to! I know it's yours and everything, but I took this thing around the last few days. It's pretty sweet." He tossed Jeremy the helmet. "You wear that, always. We clear?"

Jeremy turned the helmet over in his hands. It did seem silly and probably looked even goofier when it was on his head. He fastened the strap under his chin. "I promise."

"One more thing." Jack fished a cell phone out of his pocket. "This is yours too. I programed my number into the contacts. You know how to use this?"

Jeremy swiped around on the screen. They used tablets and laptops at the hospital. "I do."

"Not the best reception up here. A lot of calls get dropped and internet speed is pretty slow. This is something of a necessity nowadays, but our data plan is far from unlimited. So just be mindful of it. I put in an alert for us. We get close to going over…"

"I get it, Uncle Jack."

"Climb on."

Jeremy straddled the scooter. His feet were planted on the ground. Jack slapped down the visor, flashed two thumbs up.

Jeremy raised the visor. "These mean a lot to me, Uncle Jack. I really appreciate everything you've done—everything you're doing for me."

"Look. The scooter is for selfish reasons. I didn't want to hear you begging to use my truck. Figured I got to get you something to get around in. Until we teach you to drive and get you a proper license, you have this. And the phone, like I said. It's a necessity. If there were payphones on every corner I would have just given you a roll of quarters or something."

"Don't I still need a license to drive this, though?"

Jack shrugged. "I don't know. You might. We'll go to the DMV in Old Forge this week, see what's what. How does that sound?"

Jeremy turned the key. The engine purred quietly. Part of him expected a loud rumble. Smoke spurting out of the pipes.

"Sweet, huh?"

"It's pretty cool, Uncle Jack."

"Take her around for a bit. Not too far. Not too long. A lot of deer out there. They do crippling damage to cars. You hit a deer on this thing, well, I can only imagine it wouldn't be pretty." Jack pointed toward the road. "Keep the speed down and an eye out for deer. Go on. Get outta here."

Jeremy gunned the throttle. The scooter shot forward. The front wheel lifted off the ground and the rear wheel kicked up dirt and stones. Jeremy fell off the scooter, landed on his back and the air rushed out of his lungs as he gasped.

Jack fumbled for the scooter.

It righted itself, rolled a few feet and fell over.

Jack held a hand out. Jeremy took it and was hoisted up onto his feet.

"You okay?" He had Jeremy by the shoulders and was studying his body for injuries.

"I'm fine. Embarrassed." He removed the helmet.

"When I tried that thing out, same thing happened to me!"

"Really?" Jeremy tucked the helmet under an arm.

Jack nodded and then shook his head. "Nah, kid. Not really."

They laughed.

Jack clapped a hand on Jeremy's back. "I'll, uh, I'll give you some lessons tomorrow. How's that sound?"

"Good, Uncle Jack. Sounds good."

Chapter 7

Tuesday, September 6th

The sunny morning was misleading. Jeremy wasn't looking forward to the first day of work. He spent much of the morning in the bathroom, his stomach upset and didn't leave until he had nothing left to give.

Jeremy spent Sunday and Monday practicing on the scooter. He'd figured out how to ride without crashing. It might not deserve a pat on the back, but Jack made him feel good about the minor accomplishment. They cooked hotdogs on the grill Monday and kept small talk going for most of the evening.

It was as if silence made Jack apprehensive. He didn't know if Jack grew apprehensive around *just* him, or if he was that way with everyone.

Main Street had an angled front parking along the road in front of the small businesses on either side. Jeremy pulled into an empty space in front of *Danny's Diner*. It sat sandwiched between *Chahta's Hardware* and the *Fort Keeps Cinema*.

Jeremy loved the front of the diner. It looked like a silver train car.

A bell jingled as the diner's front opened. A woman in black slacks, a white dress shirt and apron stuck her head out. "You Jeremy Raines?"

"Yes, ma'am."

The woman stepped out onto the sidewalk, stood up straight. "Ma'am? Look, pull around back. That's where we park."

"Around back?"

She pointed down the street and then hooked her thumb. "Got it?"

Jeremy climbed onto his scooter. "Yes."

He left the straps loose on the helmet and made his way down to the main intersection, made the right and then an immediate right. Each business had, or shared a dumpster. A few cars were parked here and there. Jeremy found the back of *Danny's* and parked next to a rusted, white sedan.

Dressed in blue jeans and a t-shirt, Jeremy smoothed his hands down his pants and walked up to the back door. It was metal, green and closed. He knocked and took a step back. When no one answered he knocked a second time.

The door squealed as it opened. This time a man appeared. He wore a white cook's cap over dark brown, maybe black hair and a food-stained white apron over a navy blue t-shirt. Clean shaven, he looked around forty years old. "Raines?"

"Yes, sir."

"What are you knocking for?"

"To be let in."

"You work here, kid. You just open the door. C'mon in. I'll give you the fifty cent tour." The man held out a hand once Jeremy was inside. "Barry Roth."

Jeremy shook his hand.

"I run the place. My father, Danny, owns it. He's in Nevada most of the time now."

"Nice to meet you, Mr. Roth."

"Yeah. Marsha just told me about you. Call me Barry, or Roth, or Cook, or chef ... I sling hash, scramble eggs, fry burgers. Better not call me chef. I'm not really a chef. Thing is, none of this Mister and Ma'am stuff, 'kay?"

It came out harsh. Jeremy understood. It was somewhat comforting, he guessed. Less formal was better. "Okay."

"Good. I got an apron for you," he said.

The fifty cent tour could have been more clearly described as the twenty-five cent tour. "Bathrooms are over there. You keep the toilet paper and paper towel rolls filled, sweep them now and then, empty the baskets and run a mop over the tiles at the end of the night. Sound simple?"

"Yes." He chomped teeth down on his tongue, biting off *sir*.

Barry crossed his arms. "Yeah, well it ain't. People are slobs. Can have nothing but men and women wearing business suits in here and come the end of the day, those bathrooms will be wrecked. Wads of balled up this and that on the floor and urine all over the place. Slobs. Every last one of them. Makes you wonder what their homes look like. It's all I'm sayin'."

They passed through a single swinging door into the dining area.

Barry said, "Marsha you've met."

"Not officially." Marsha wore her auburn hair up and away from her face except for small curly wisps that fell near her ears. Long crimson red fingernails matched glossed over lipstick. Marsha reminded Jeremy of one of the nurses at the hospital, Kendra. They both had soft brown eyes and a narrow nose, which made Marsha around thirty.

Jeremy nodded. "Nice to meet you."

"You go by Jeremy? Jer? Raines?"

He shrugged, shaking his head. "It doesn't matter to me. Jeremy's fine."

"Yeah? Well, good. Same for me. I prefer Marsha. Not Marsh. My mother calls me Marsh. Eats right through me when she does it and infuriates me when anyone else tries it." She poked at her hair with a pencil. "It's not like the worst thing in the world if it slips out, but do us both a favor and don't let it slip out."

"Marsha." It was like he was trying it out for a test ride.

"We have another waitress, works dinner shift, Allana," Barry said. "You'll meet her later. But basically, we have the twelve floor mounted stools along the counter, we've got the six booths along the front wall, we can serve up to thirty people at a time in here. Rare we ever have that many. Summer weekends, yeah. Sundays for breakfast and lunch after church, yeah. Rest of the time, not so much. Back here behind the counter is where Marsha and Allana do the prep work, make coffee, desserts and that kind of thing. You and me, we're rarely in the dining area. See the jukeboxes on the tables? Just for show. Was a time when they worked. We got the jukebox on the wall over there, but it's digital. It takes cash, but mostly kids pre-load money on a phone app, select and play songs that way. You and me, we're the behind the scenes of the place." Barry waved Jeremy over. "Come with me and we'll get your paperwork done."

Jeremy followed Barry around back. Dividing the prep work counter and the grill was a stainless steel window for orders placed and orders up. A silver call bell sat beside a large spatula.

"You like that? That there is my sixty inch four gas burner range with a thirty-sixty inch griddle. Not top of the line, or new, but I keep her clean and she works perfectly for me." Barry stood for a moment and admired his stove. "It has two twenty-six wide, twenty-six and a half deep inch ovens that will heat up to five hundred degrees in the snap of a finger."

Jeremy was at a loss. "Cool."

Seemed to work. Barry nodded. "Very cool."

The office was opposite the kitchen area.

"Your Uncle Jack's a good friend of mine. We grew up together," Barry said. He sat in a chair at a steel desk that faced a wall. An old computer with a big, heavy monitor shared space with stacks of papers. Two four drawer filing cabinets stood behind him. A cork board with a scheduling calendar was on the wall and in one corner a mounted rack with aprons and navy blue *Danny's Diner* t-shirts. "I knew your father, too. He was a good man."

"Thank you." It sounded flat, hollow. Jeremy had never spent time wondering about how other people might have known his parents.

"Yeah, well. Anyway, I like how you got here early today," Barry said. "But from now on, plan on coming in around eleven, eleven-thirty even. We close at nine, after clean-up, we're out by nine-thirty, ten at the latest. It's a long day, but you'll get a small cut of tips on top of what I pay you. You get time and a half for anything over forty hours. We good with that?"

"We're good."

"Your main thing will be keeping up on dishes. Glasses. Silverware. I don't have a fancy machine. I have a big two-tub stainless steel sink. When you get in they'll be stacked. I don't want you knocking at the door. It's unlocked as long as I'm here. You come in, throw on an apron and get to work. You wash dishes, scrub pots and pans and if I need you for anything else, I'll call for you. It's not glamorous, but it's good, honest work.

"Now, I want you to fill out these, your W-2 and such and then you can get started, or if you want, you can come back fresh tomorrow. Your call."

"I'd like to start right away, if it's alright?"

"More than alright. Keep up on the breakfast dishes and it won't seem so busy the rest of the day." Barry stood up. He grabbed a folded diner shirt and apron off the rack. "These are yours. Have a seat. I'll be on the grill. Just leave the paperwork on the computer keyboard and I'll get it taken care of."

Chapter 8

Jeremy pulled up into the driveway. The split level was simple. Second story bedrooms sat over the garage. Once inside and to the right was the family room, toward the back the kitchen and a sunporch. He parked the scooter in the garage and then dragged himself into the house.

"That was a long first day." Jack sat on the couch, feet crossed on an ottoman, laptop on his legs, the television remote in one hand, a glass of milk in the other. "I left you dinner wrapped in the microwave. Isn't much."

"Barry said the job's basically from eleven until close."

"Days off?"

Jeremy dropped into the recliner, but sat forward on the edge. "He didn't say."

"Going to want to get that cleared up. Nothing wrong with working hard, but you don't need to be there seven days a week. He stands to inherit the place. That's his reason for working twenty-four-seven. Earning minimum wage is why you deserve time off." Jack winked. "I'm sure he just forgot to go over that with you. Still worth asking about tomorrow."

"I will." Jeremy stood up. "Is it okay if I eat dinner later? I'm looking forward to a shower and some sleep."

"Absolutely."

Jeremy held up a bag. "Barry made you a burger and fries. No charge, he said."

Jack dropped the remote onto the couch cushion, leaned forward and snatched the brown bag out of Jeremy's hand. "Thought that's what I smelled. This is going to be nice having you work at the diner. Want half?"

"No, thank you." Jeremey held up both hands and backed away slowly. "I just want to shower and get some sleep."

"Have at it." Jack replied almost out of obligation. He was elbows deep in the brown bag, removing a wax paper wrapped burger and then unwrapped the fries. He took a big bite of the burger. "I guess I won't see you in the morning, so, have a good night."

* * *

Jeremy stayed in the shower for a dangerously long time; he rocked back and forth on his feet and his eyelids grew heavier. The massaging water spray was putting him to sleep while standing up. The steam filled the bathroom from the ceiling down.

The sound of a door closing snapped him out of the daze.

"Uncle Jack?"

Even through the steamed glass shower door, Jeremy could make out the dark, solid shape of someone stooped over the sink, as if they were looking into the mirror.

He swiped a hand across the etched glass, but with privacy design couldn't see anything more than an inky form.

"Uncle Jack?" Jeremy didn't want to raise his voice. It came out hesitant, just above a whisper, but was enough.

The head of *whatever* it was swiveled around.

Whoever it was, they were looking at him.

Jeremy stumbled backward, his feet slid in the wet acrylic tub. He lost his balance and his shoulder blades smacked the wall tiles. His right hand shot out and latched onto the shower head. The angle shift. Hot water sprayed his thighs as more steam filled up the bathroom.

The thing came at the glass fast, hard. "You're not going anywhere!"

The voice was rushed, gravely, but low. It sounded as if what he'd heard had actually been whispered in his ears, up close. Personal.

The form pressed against the shower doors. Blackness spread and crept up over the top in wisps like hundreds of long thin fingers.

Jeremy pressed palms against his ears and dropped into a back corner of the tub. He didn't want to hear the voice anymore, not ever again. The black form rose above the shower doors, it floated over his cowering body like a canopy in the wind.

Unable to close his eyes, or look away, unable to find his own voice so he could scream, Jeremy watched as the form swirled around over him before it swooped down and blanketed his wet and now shivering body.

The bathroom door banged open.

"Jeremy?"

Uncle Jack?

Jeremy saw through the darkness as the darkness became suddenly translucent, then clear and light filled the room.

The steam mostly dissipated.

The glass door was rolled open. Turning off the water, Jack said, "Jeremy! What happened?"

"Slipped and fell."

"Did you hit your head?"

Jeremy wanted a towel. "I just need help getting up."

"That water was hot, but you're ice cold." Jack got his nephew up onto his feet and handed over a towel. "You're shivering."

"Think I used all the hot water." His legs were pink and felt raw. He'd be surprised if he didn't have some second degree burns.

"Come on, let me help you out."

Jack led Jeremy to his room. Jeremy read the expression on his uncle's face. The man wanted to know if something was wrong. He deserved an answer, too.

Jeremy had no intention of sharing what happened in the bathroom just now with anyone.

He'd be back in St. Mary's before morning.

37

"I was tired. I slipped. I've always been a bit of a klutz. Don't see why now should be any different." It was the best he could offer. None of what he said was a lie.

"Can I get you anything?" Jack's eyes went to the nightstand.

Jeremy never expected he'd work such a long day. He was a few hours late on his meds.

That could be the issue, but didn't reach for them like a junky, or his uncle might suspect something *was* wrong. "I'm just gonna put something on and get to sleep."

"Okay," Jack said, "I think I am gonna turn in, too."

Once Jeremy was alone inside his room, he threw on a pair of shorts and a tank top. He opened the bedroom window for a breeze that didn't exist and climbed into bed.

He stayed still and stared silently at the hallway light peeking from under the door.

A shadow blocked the light. Moved past the door to the right, toward Uncle Jack's room.

Jeremy sighed.

The shadow returned. Jeremy sat up straight in bed. He kept telling himself that this wasn't happening. The shadow went left this time.

There was a soft *cli*-click. The hallway went dark.

Jeremy couldn't tell who was standing outside the door. He heard floorboards creak. "Good night, Jer. Hope you have a good day at work tomorrow."

"Thanks Uncle Jack. You, too."

Jeremy dropped back onto his pillow. His uncle must be second guessing the decision on letting him move back home. The last thing he wanted to do was cause trouble for him, or anyone. He looked up at the ceiling for just a moment before deciding, despite the heat and humidity, sleeping with the blanket over his head made the most sense.

Chapter 9

Fort Keeps, NY — Adirondacks — October 1912

"As long as you don't mind, Elissa, you can ride with me." Sheriff O'Sullivan sat in the saddle and held out a hand. The mane of his brown mare was fresh cut and groomed. A rifle was holstered and dangled from straps slung over the ends of the saddle.

Toughest part of his job involved delivering bad news. The death of a child was worst of all. Bringing Elissa out to view the body was merely a formality. He'd known Alice since she'd been a tot and remembered visiting a time or two and seeing Alice sitting in tall grass while her mother hung laundry on the line.

Although she stayed in a nightgown, Elissa had bundled herself inside a long wool coat and turned up the collar. Should keep her warm, unless the wind picks up. Night was cold enough he saw his own breath.

She looked toward her barn.

"Save you the trouble of disturbing your horses," O'Sullivan said. The horse shook its head and its ears twitched. He loved how she seemed in tune with his thoughts. Best horse he'd ever had. He leaned forward and patted the mare's muscular neck.

"I suppose it will be alright."

He reached out for her again and she locked her hand on his forearm. He hoisted her up and onto the horse, so she sat on the back of the saddle behind him.

"You okay?"

"As can be expected." She sounded tired, frail. The sheriff thought he caught a tremble in her tone of voice.

"Hold tight." He gave the mare a kick, slapped the reins and she trotted away from Elissa's place. It was as fast as he'd push her. The ground was hard and piles of fallen leaves held moisture. If she slipped and became maimed, he'd never forgive himself. Navigation in the mountains was challenging enough during ideal conditions.

A crisp white moon lit the night above tall, bare trees. The forest was alive with the sounds of night. Hordes of crickets chirped and frogs croaked. Overhead, there came the occasional screech of bats and the unmistakable flutter of their flapping wings; the hunt for insects was on.

Sheriff O'Sullivan left one deputy at the scene, watching over the body and sent a second to fetch the doctor.

Death happened in the Adirondacks, only the cause was more often natural than not. His first year as sheriff two men fought inside the local tavern. Gregory Finn beat Trevin Smart near to death after breaking the man's arm. The bartender broke up the fight, sent Finn home. Someone ran for the doc. Smart lived, but nearly lost his job at the mill. Tough getting work done with an arm in a sling for six weeks. Roughly two weeks after the fight, Finn's home was invaded. The scoundrels hogtied his family and left them in one of the back bedrooms. The doc believed different blunt objects were used to beat Finn to death before hanging him from the oak in front of the house. Didn't take O'Sullivan long rounding up suspects. Smart's two older brothers were known hotheads and seeking revenge on their kid brother didn't take much effort. The Smarts confessed, were tried and sentenced to life in the Eastern State Penitentiary in Pennsylvania. Near complete isolation kept the brothers from any interaction within, or outside of the prisons' walls. The entire affair was resolved in less than a month from the initial fight.

That happened a little more than ten years ago. Hadn't been a murder since. This death didn't sit right with O'Sullivan. Alice was thirteen, fourteen years old. The corpse was naked. Scratches and bruising looked like they may have occurred post death.

Ahead, lanterns hung on tree branches. Three men stood around the body.

Sheriff O'Sullivan sucked in a deep breath, as he tugged on the reins. His mare slowed. He helped Elissa off the horse. She held onto his arm, as she slid down.

He dismounted and holding the reins in one hand, said, "Now, I need you to prepare yourself."

Elissa's eyes were open wide; tears streaked down the corners, wetting her cheeks. Her mouth was drawn into a frown and her lips quivered. "I don't think I can go over there. I, I'm not sure I can do this."

"We'll go over together." The other men were huddled together, they stood in front of the corpse and stared at the sheriff and Elissa. "Then I'll take you back home."

He watched Elissa mull over the words. There wasn't much choice. She was here, she would identify the body and he would take her home. His investigation was just beginning, as was the end of her world. It didn't seem just, or fair. Life happened that way sometimes. It was horrible when it caught someone unexpected; when it left someone helpless and feeling hopeless.

"Elissa," he said. He spoke softly, giving her a gentle nudge and she responded. They took baby steps.

She held onto his arm, tight, but walked directly behind him. He knew she used his body as a shield. Nothing would keep the truth out of her eyes. The nightmares would haunt her for the rest of her life. If there was something he could do to prevent the pain and suffering about to be bestowed upon this poor woman, he would. There was not a thing that could be done.

Except justice.

He could vow to find the person or those responsible.

Sometimes closure brought about a certain amount of peace. And sometimes it did absolutely nothing.

The men removed their hats, held them respectfully against their chests and parted, giving the sheriff and Elissa full view of the body.

Elissa turned away and clung to the sheriff. She gripped his shirt in both hands and cried into his chest.

"That's Alice! That's my daughter!"

Chapter 10

Wednesday, September 7th

Barry Roth locked the diner doors. "Good job tonight, Jeremy."

Jeremy was exhausted. The stacks of dirty dishes kept coming. The heat from the ovens, the hot water and the day suffocated him. His clothing, wet with sweat stuck to his body. He couldn't wait to get home and shower. The thought of ice cold water raining down on his head made him smile. He climbed onto his scooter and pulled the helmet on over his head. "Thank you."

"You be careful on that thing. Lot of deer out this time of year."

"Yes, sir."

Roth shot Jeremy a look.

"Barry. Yes, Barry. I will," he said, starting the engine with his key.

Barry climbed into a pick-up truck and pulled out of the parking lot while Jeremy adjusted the straps under his chin. He was overheated. The helmet wasn't helping. Part of him thought it worth the risk to ride without one. His uncle would kill him if he were caught.

He heard a commotion coming from the street. He edged his way up to the edge of the back lot and looked both ways. Not seeing anything, he drove toward Main Street. Parked in front of one of the shops, a woman fought off a man.

Jeremy's stomach dropped.

The guy had the woman by the arm. The passenger door of a vehicle was open. "Get in the car, Greta. Now."

Jeremy looked left and right. No one was around was to help her. Except him.

"Kevin, stop! Stop it!"

Jeremy rolled up. Feet planted. Hands on the handlebars. "What's going on here?"

Kevin spun around, releasing Greta.

"What'd you say?" Kevin stood close to six feet tall, dark blond hair buzzed military style. He wore loose jeans and a too tight gray rock band t-shirt that accentuated muscles earned from endless hours in a gym.

"Just, ah, asking what's going on here."

"What's it look like?" Kevin's hands were balled into fists.

"To me, it looks like you're trying to force this girl into your car." Jeremy arched his eyebrows. "And she doesn't want to go."

"Tell you what. Why don't you get out of here? Ride your moped home and I'll ignore the fact you're sticking your nose in my business." Kevin turned around, facing Greta.

"It's her business, too." Jeremy stared at Greta. Her eyes never left him. She looked as if she were silently pleading for help.

Kevin turned back. "What?"

"I'm good with you wanting me to leave." He pointed at Greta. "But what does she want?"

"I'll go with him," she said. Long, straight dark hair went well past her shoulders. Some was tucked behind her left ear. Big, brown eyes looked focused on him. "Everything's okay."

"See that?" Kevin said. "Misunderstanding. Now get lost."

"Are you sure you're okay?" Jeremy asked Greta.

She walked up to the car, rested her hands on the open door. "I'm okay. Thank you."

Kevin went around to the driver's side. "You, get in the car." He pointed at Jeremy. "And you, get lost, got me?"

* * *

Jeremy parked his scooter in the garage. Adrenaline like electricity coursed through his body. His upset stomach turned over inside his gut sending bile up his throat. It burned, but he was thankful he hadn't puked.

He shouldn't have let things go. Greta didn't want to get in the car. It seemed like she only did so to keep him from getting stomped by Kevin. *She* rescued him, not the other way around.

Inside the house, candlelight came from the kitchen.

Jeremy spent as little time as possible inside the kitchen. The memories of that room came back in waves that left him off balance and feeling nauseated. His stomach already sour, he wasn't sure he wanted to go into the room. "Uncle Jack?"

He heard a noise. A glass against glass clink.

Jeremy set his helmet down on the sofa. "Uncle Jack?"

Unable to shake the sensation he was being watched, he looked up the stairs on his left. The hallway at the top was dark. He thought someone was standing in that darkness looking down at him.

Motionless, he waited.

If something moved, he was running out of the house.

He heard another clink.

It came from the kitchen. There was another sound. A sob.

"Uncle Jack?" Jeremy's mouth went dry. He wasn't sure he was calling out for his uncle or whispering. He took tentative steps forward.

He saw on the center of the table two lit candles. The flames danced. Shadows flickered on the walls.

Another step.

Seated at the table, a bottle of whiskey and a shot glass in front of him, was Jack. His elbow was on the table, his lowered head resting in the crook of a hand.

"Uncle Jack, are you alright?"

The living room connected to the kitchen. A cabinet and refrigerator were directly in front. Beyond those was the door leading out back. To the right was the table. Around it was counter space, the sink and above the sink, a window.

Jeremy saw blood on the curtains and counter.

There was more blood on the table and floor.

A chair was overturned.

His mother was dead between the table and the counter.

At her feet was his father. Dead.

Jeremy froze.

"I didn't hear you come in."

There was a knife on the floor, beside his mother's lifeless body. He could smell urine and feces.

"Jeremy?"

Jeremy blinked.

The kitchen was not covered in blood. The bodies of his parents were not strewn about the floor.

A chair slid across linoleum.

Jack stood up. "I didn't mean for you to see me this way."

"Are you okay?" His uncle had been crying.

"Want to sit for a minute?"

Jeremy didn't. What he wanted was that cold shower, but for different reason now. The sweat and grime from work was nearly forgotten.

Jack pulled out a chair. "Sit."

There wasn't much of a choice. Jeremy sat, while Jack opened a cupboard and removed a glass.

Sitting at the table, Jack refilled his glass and poured two fingers for Jeremy. "Ever have whiskey before?"

He'd been locked away in an institution since he was eight years old. "I haven't."

Jack smiled, pushing the glass in front of his nephew. "It's an acquired taste."

Jeremy watched his uncle down the honey-brown alcohol in his own glass in a gulp.

"I was just sitting here. I do that sometimes. And I let it get to me," Jack said.

Jeremy ignored the double shot of whiskey. "Let what get to you?"

"The past. My brother. I just wish I knew what could have been going through his mind."

Jeremy didn't need any clarifying questions. He would never forget the day he found his parents dead.

"I still don't believe it. Any of it. But mostly, my brother wasn't a killer. He loved your mom. He loved her. He would never have laid as much as a hand on her. And then to take his own life? He didn't own a gun, a handgun. I just can't understand how it all happened."

It was late at night. Mid-summer. He'd woken to the sound of his parents fighting. He heard a struggle. Raised voiced. Making his way out of bedroom and down the hall, he knew something was wrong when everything went silent.

At the bottom of the staircase, he looked around and into the kitchen.

And then he saw the gun.

Heard the shot.

His father's body dropped, knocking over a chair.

He froze.

"I'm sorry. This can't be any easier for you," Jack said. "Hell, I know it's not. And that breaks my heart, too. That you were the one to find them that way."

Jeremy thought about getting up and going outside. He felt his chest tighten. Breathing became labored. "I need some air."

His legs didn't respond, as he continued sitting at the table.

Jack refilled his glass. "I'm sorry."

"I just need some air." With tremendous effort, Jeremy pushed back the chair and stood up.

He didn't want to go out the back door. Something about it bothered him. It was as if part of his memory had something to do with that back door and his mind wasn't ready for the exposure.

The back door.

Jeremy fled the kitchen, ran through the living room and out the front door.

The air felt cool, almost cold against his skin. Clouds covered most of the moon. It was as if his ears popped and he could hear more clearly. More crickets. More frogs. The leaves rustled as a breeze passed through the branches.

He bent forward and placed his hands on his knees. He had trouble catching his breath. His medications were in his room and he was late taking them again.

This isn't working out, he thought. *I should go back to St. Mary's. I shouldn't be here. I shouldn't be home.*

Chapter 11

Jeremy concentrated on the dishes. It kept more than his hands busy. If he focused on every motion he made, the sponge passing over dried and caked on food, the time went faster. He kept the water hot and filled with suds and always saved the silverware for last. Dirty dishes and filthy pots and pans were still better than washing silverware.

Barry needed a dishwasher. Not a person. A machine. The investment had to be cheaper over time than hiring someone for the labor. Jeremy kept his mouth shut. He was thankful for the work.

Mostly.

With a G.E.D. he wondered if this was it. Would life have anything else to offer? Would he spend the rest of his life living with his uncle, in his parents' old house, while he made a meager living washing dishes? Having only been home a few days, it was far too early to assess the rest of his life. There was an entire world beyond Fort Keeps.

Once he turned eighteen, he could do whatever he wanted. Only that was part of the problem. He had no idea what it was he wanted to do. He couldn't recall what he wanted to be when he grew up. A cop, maybe. Or a fireman?

At eight years old, did kids dream of becoming things like an accountant or a dentist? Did it matter? Getting a good job required a college education. Jeremy did pretty well when taking classes inside the hospital. He always received above average grades. The G.E.D. test had been simple. Maybe college wasn't out of reach.

With a college degree he knew he'd only be stuck in Fort Keeps for a short while; it would be temporary and not permanent.

The swinging door swung open. "Jeremy!"

Jeremy went rigid; the muscles in his shoulders and back tensed as if struck in the back of the head. He dropped the sponge into the sink.

Barry said, "Didn't mean to scare you."

"It's alright."

"Look, sheriff's here to see you. I asked him to come around back," he said.

"What's he want?" Jeremy lifted the top of his apron strap over his head.

Barry looked back, toward the diner, before stepping through the doorway. "I was hoping you could tell me. Your uncle and I go back. This is a favor to him, okay? So far, you're working out. You're on time. You do a solid job. But I can't have the police coming around here. Can you see what I'm saying?"

"I do, Barry."

"You in some kind a trouble? Want me to call down the street, have Jack come on up?"

Jeremy shook his head. "No. I haven't done anything wrong. I haven't even been anywhere except here and home."

Barry tried smiling. Looked more grimace-like. "Okay, kid. I'm just putting it out there. Police start showing up, I gotta let you go. That's just life."

"I'm sure this is nothing or some misunderstanding."

There was knock at the back door. It stood wide open. If there was any wind at all the breeze wasn't making it into the back of the diner, or there would be some much needed relief from the heat.

The sheriff stood in the threshold in tan work boots, mud brown slacks and a khaki shirt. The five-star gold badge looked recently polished. The black leather belt sagged on the right hip. The butt of a gun protruded from the holster.

Jeremy's breath caught in his chest. His anxiety kicked in. Spreading his fingers out sometimes helped. So did removing clothing. The sensation came over him like claustrophobia.

"So the rumors *are* true," the sheriff said.

"We all set here, sheriff?" Barry asked, looking suspiciously at Jeremy. "You okay, kid?"

The sheriff was grinning. "I'll just take a minute of his time, show myself out when I'm done."

Barry nodded. "Okay. Sure."

When the swinging door stopped swinging, the sheriff said, "Had a run in with a young couple last night, I hear."

The words sounded muffled. Jeremy's heart beat fast and hard. The throb echoed inside his head, pounded between his ears. "Did the lady file a report?"

"Lady?" the sheriff said, under his breath. "No. Kevin O'Sullivan informed me of the incident."

Jeremy was surprised. "Oh. Well, that's good, I guess."

"Good, you guess?" He snickered. "Not sure how you see that as good. But maybe that's just how your brain works, all twisted and abnormal."

Jeremy shook his head. "I'm not understanding."

"No. I don't suppose you are. Look, your uncle wanted you home. You're the last of the family and all of that. I get it. I do. But this here is a small town. We're not used to having trouble makers. I don't know if you needed more time in the ward, or what. I just want to make one thing clear."

Jeremy didn't like the tone of the conversation. The sheriff took steps toward him; hand on the butt of his gun. "I think you may have some incorrect information, sir."

The sheriff stopped him. Both hands up. Palms facing Jeremy. "Listen to me, kid. If I ever catch wind that you're harassing people again, anyone, it's not going to end well for you. If that happens, when I'm done with you, you'll be wishing you still had a nice room with the crazies. Where you'll wind up is in a jail cell. Prison. You got it?"

"Sir—"

"Do you get me?"

There was no winning the talk. Jeremy knew better than to keep at it. Resolved, he nodded.

"Say it."

"I get you."

"I'm going to be keeping an eye on you, Raines. You might not see me, but I'll be there. Remember that." Without another word, the sheriff turned around and left.

Jeremy's body shook.

The swinging door swung open. Barry stood with arms crossed.

"I didn't do anything, I swear." Jeremy felt the need to defend himself.

Barry's lips pursed. "I know. I know it now. Had a run in with Kevin O'Sullivan?"

Jeremy nodded. "He was fighting with a girl."

"Greta Murray. His girlfriend. The two have been on again off again all during high school. You know who the sheriff is?"

He looked familiar. Something about the man struck a chord inside Jeremy's head. It left his insides trembling. "No. Should I?"

"Christopher O'Sullivan. Kevin's father. Comes from a long line of sheriffs in this town, dating as far back as the mid eighteen-hundreds."

Chapter 12

Sheriff O'Sullivan couldn't get warm. Fresh coffee perked over an open flame on the iron stove. He blew into cupped hands and then tucked them under his arms. "So what do we have here?"

"Trying to determine a time of death." Dr. John Marr had Alice on his examination table. With his gold spectacles low on his nose, the man squinted as he lifted up an arm. "I believe she is still in the stages of rigor mortis, despite how cold the body is and not algor mortis. I suspect the Crosby girl has been dead between three to eight hours and no more. Also, I've checked under her fingernails, but didn't find much of anything."

O'Sullivan poured himself a mug of coffee, then held it with both hands, appreciative of the warmth provided. "I don't see why her fingernails are relevant."

Marr removed his glasses. "If she fought off an attacker, there'd likely be skin, or blood under the nails." He pantomimed clawing at the air.

The sheriff raised an eyebrow, shrugging. "And what good is blood or skin under the fingernails going to do us?"

"Gives you something to start with. If I can prove she fought back, then maybe looking for someone with fresh scratches narrows the search. Maybe they have marks across their face or down their arm."

"I like that. Very clever." O'Sullivan sipped his coffee and nodded. "This is good doc," he said.

"Thank you. I attribute it to cleaning the kettle everyday." Marr smiled. "How was the body discovered?"

"We didn't touch or move her until you arrived."

Marr shook his head. "I mean how, who found her?"

"Parsons was hiking with his dogs. One of his labs must have picked up the scent. He said they led him right to Alice."

"Anything off about his story?" Marr asked.

"Man's nearly seventy. Walks the mountains with his dogs every night. Never takes the same paths twice." O'Sullivan shrugged. "I'm not ruling out anyone as a potential suspect at this point. With Parsons, I just don't see it."

Marr said, "Parsons. Yeah. I agree. I don't see it."

"Okay. So aside from not finding anything under her nails, what have you found?"

Marr replaced his glasses. They sat higher on the bridge of his nose, but as the doctor leaned forward and lifted the girl's head, they slid away from his eyes. "You can see here, under the matt of hair."

"That blood?"

"Dried. Her skull is fractured. Brain must have swelled. Internal bleeding."

"That what killed her?" O'Sullivan stepped back, away from the body. Alice's skin was blue, bruised. She looked stiff and doll-like. His eyes kept finding her chest. A crazy part of him kept expecting it would rise and fall, as if she were alive and breathing.

"Seems like it."

"And the scratches and marks on her body?" O'Sullivan set his mug down. As much as he didn't like the idea, he took a closer look at Alice's legs and torso. He pointed at a spot. "I mean this, on the back of her thigh—"

"The bite marks?"

"It's more than bite marks, doc. Something *ate* a chunk out of her leg." O'Sullivan inadvertently wiped his hand down the front of his shirt, even though he'd had no direct contact with the corpse.

"There's no telling how long she was out in the woods. After just a first examination, I'd wager something like a raccoon is the culprit."

"A raccoon?"

"Don't hold me to it. I've measured the size of the area and recorded it. Seems too small a circumference for a man, woman, or child for that matter. I wouldn't say it resembled a human bite at all." Dr. John Marr walked around the body and lifted his mug of coffee. "Why don't you head home, sheriff. There's nothing you can do here. If I find out anything earth-shattering, I'll come by your house, otherwise, stop back in the morning."

Benji O'Sullivan chewed on his lip.

"Is there something else, sheriff?"

O'Sullivan pointed at Alice, words fumbled around in his mind for a moment while he did his best at formulating a question. "I need to know. Was anything else done to her?"

Marr pursed his lips, but shook his head. "I did an examination. Her hymen was still intact. That in and of itself doesn't mean she hadn't been sexually active or that she hadn't been raped. But I also didn't find any signs of activity around the vagina. So the answer is no. I do not believe Elissa's little girl was raped."

The sheriff sighed. That was one less thing. Once words spread of Alice's murder, he'd have his hands full. If she had been raped, that would only further enrage the people. "That's good, doc. I'm real glad to hear that. Real glad."

There was no way he could go home. Sleep would be impossible. He tipped his hat, left his coffee and went out into the night.

His mare waited for him; her reins wrapped around a post. "Hey, girl," he said and patted the side of her face.

As he climbed up onto the saddle, he knew where his investigation would begin. Alice had been found on the Gregory land. While he wasn't ruling anyone out, he didn't think Mr. Gregory was responsible.

His boys, on the other hand, have been a bit more rowdy than most, as of late. They were a year or two older than Alice. Hormones ran fast and hard in boys that age.

Chapter 13

Thursday Night, September 8th

Jeremy couldn't sleep. He sat in bed with his back to the wall. The window was open a crack. The cool night air felt refreshing. While the curtains swayed from the breeze, an aroma from a nearby wood burning stove entered the room. The only light came from a sliver of moonbeam visible on the floor.

He elected to not tell his uncle about the encounter with the sheriff. Still affected by the death of his brother and sister-in-law, Jeremy didn't want any more burden falling onto Jack's shoulders. The solution was keeping away from Kevin and his father. Head down, he'd do his best to go unnoticed. In the ward, it had been simple. Invisibility was achievable and sustainable. He'd reached that level of insignificance easily. The staff spent time on patients demanding attention and that was around the clock.

Jeremy dropped elbows onto raised knees and buried his face in his hands. Exhausted, after a long and stressful shift, sleep should not be evading him. The one highlight was that Barry believed he hadn't done anything wrong. Everything could have gone south fast if his boss took sides with the sheriff. He was the new person in town, the outsider.

No. That wasn't true.

Born and raised in Fort Keeps, he was every bit a resident as they were. *Kind of.*

A floorboard moaned.

Jeremy dropped his hands away from his face. With eyes wide open he scanned the room. Moving away from the moonbeam of light were nothing but darker and darker shades of black.

The corners of the room were so dark, they looked as if there were no boundaries. He feared if he worked up courage to walk into a corner he would not find any wall; feared he'd walk on and on into other rooms, reach other realms, cross over to parallel worlds.

He wasn't moving. Nothing would make him get out of bed.

It was a floorboard. Nothing more. Houses made settling noises. Even old houses. *Especially* old houses.

He was tired. This was what happened when his body needed, but refused sleep.

The bottles of pills on his nightstand taunted him.

He couldn't recall if he'd taken his prescriptions. There was no way he forgot them, he knew he craved them by the time he arrived home from work. At the moment, though, he just couldn't remember.

Another moan.

Was that the floorboard, again?

It didn't sound like it. Not this time.

Every part of his being urged him to close his eyes. Hiding under blankets had helped before. There was no reason it wouldn't work this time, too.

He stared at the floor just past the foot of his bed, where the moonlight reached as far as it could into the room, battled futility against the growing darkness. His mind convinced him that standing in that patch of light would save him.

His life wasn't in danger.

It's just a noise. Nothing more.

He thought his arms might be getting ready to throw back the blankets, his legs preparing to make a run for it.

This was crazy. If he chanced getting out of bed, he wouldn't stop running once embraced by a moonbeam. He'd make it to the door.

The handle wouldn't turn, though.

The door would be frozen closed.

No. He shook his head. There was no reason the door wouldn't open. And yet, he convinced himself otherwise. It was now a seed of doubt. Planted. If something was in the room with him—and there wasn't, there absolutely wasn't—then he was trapped.

Except for the window.

No. He continued shaking his head. If he leapt out the window, his uncle would have no choice but to return him to St. Mary's.

I'm not going to jump out of the window!

The door would open. If he needed to flee the room, the door would open.

Instead of reacting at all, Jeremy stayed silent in bed.

He wasn't sure how much time passed. His phone was on the dresser, charging.

He counted inside his head. One, two, three, four.

When he reached three hundred, he stopped. This was already out of hand. Ludicrous. This was his house. His room.

There was nothing to be scared of.

Whatever he saw, *or thought he saw*, when he first arrived home was explainable. Returning was traumatic and clearly rekindled some unwanted memories. He knew he still had ... *things* ... wedged inside of his mind.

Something was close to wiggling free earlier today, at the diner. A snapshot, a painful memory perhaps better left stuck where it was. Enough stress had been dished out. His mind must have recognized his limitations, and let him be.

For that, he'd been thankful.

All the time spent in one-on-ones and in group sessions at St. Mary's touched at corners of so many pushed-down and pushed-aside emotions, that even in the nine years of therapy received, not everything he'd gone through on that terrible night was brought to light. Perhaps not everything would get revealed, ever. He didn't know and wasn't sure how he felt about that.

Did he need to remember everything to fully recover?

The medication next to him was a sign he wasn't at one-hundred percent. The realization made him quite apprehensive.

The sounds. The shadows. The ghost.

How could he not question his own sanity? He'd be crazy not to.

His eyelids fluttered and he fought it. For a while longer.

The lingering silence eased him into a sense of safety that if he were more alert, might not have worked.

As sleep overtook him, as his eyes began closing, he saw movement in the shadows; an even darker *form* moving across the room toward the moonlight.

His eyes opened.

She was nose to nose in front of him. She had a cracked, white face. A cloud, thick like milk, was coated over bloodshot, blue eyes. "Where is she?"

Since he had fallen asleep sitting up, Jeremy couldn't back away. To escape the woman, he tumbled left and fell out of bed.

On his belly on the floor, he looked up when he heard the woman scream.

She had jumped for him, landed on the bed. Arms and head came over the side. She reached for him. Bony fingers, with long, green and dirt covered fingernails snapped at his head.

He pushed himself across the floor, rolled over and on all fours, scrambled for the door. He couldn't help looking back.

She pulled herself off the bed and chased after him.

He grabbed the doorknob. His heart pounded so hard he feared it might explode inside his chest. Knew it might, if the door was locked.

The handle twisted.

The door opened and he stumbled forward, out of the room, trying to get his legs under him.

Her hand shot out of the room, locked around his ankle.

She brought him down. He slammed a knee on the floor and thought the kneecap shattered. Ignoring the pain radiating through his leg, he clawed his way forward, kicking at the woman with his free leg.

"Uncle Jack! Uncle Jack!"

He winced as fingernails cut into his flesh. He used all of his strength, but she was winning. He was being dragged back into the room.

He splayed his arms, left and right, catching a hold of the door frame.

A cold, clammy hand clutched each leg. It felt as if, while she pulled, she was also climbing up onto him.

Clothing rubbed over his calves. He heard her breathing and felt her breath on his back.

A door down the hall opened.

Light from the bedroom spilled into the hallway.

"Jeremy! What's going on!"

She was gone. Just like that. Gone.

Jeremy didn't risk getting taken. He clambered out of the room, struggle to get to his feet. He lost his balance and banged into the wall. "She's in there! She's in the room!"

Jack came out of his bedroom. "Who's in there?"

All Jeremy could do was point.

Without hesitation, Jack went into the Jeremy's bedroom and flipped on the light. "There's no one here. What did you see?"

It was a nightmare. It had to have been nothing more than a nightmare.

Jeremy's mouth was dry. His tongue felt thick and puffed out inside his mouth. "I'm sorry, Uncle Jack."

His uncle stood still for a moment. He looked around the bedroom and then at his nephew. "It's okay, man. Maybe bringing you back here wasn't such a good idea."

"No. It was. It's okay, I just had a bad dream—"

"Jeremy."

"I don't want to go back to St. Mary's." He hadn't realized he felt that way until now. Living in Fort Keeps was better than being in the hospital. "I'll do better. I won't disturb you anym—"

"Jer. I didn't mean taking you out of the hospital. I don't regret that. I meant bringing you back to this house. Maybe that was a bad idea."

Jeremy wasn't sure how to respond, because he wasn't sure if it had been a good idea, either, so he didn't say a word.

Chapter 14

Monday, September 19th

Trouble waited outside for Jeremy.

She looked beautiful, and even though talking to Greta Murray could be a mistake, she was waiting for him in the driveway.

"Hey," she said.

He nodded a hello.

"I would have come by sooner." She wore a navy blue hoodie under a white, puffy vest. Straight hair was still tucked behind one ear. She swayed back and forth with hands stuffed into blue jeans.

Why was she here at all, was what Jeremy wondered.

"I only just found out that Kevin told his father you harassed us," she said.

"It's okay." Warning signs, like red flares, flashed behind his eyeballs. "Just glad everything's better between you and your boyfriend."

She stopped swaying. "He's not my boyfriend. I broke up with him that night you saw us. He wasn't listening to me. Kept insisting we were still together."

"It's none of my business." Jeremy walked past her and lifted the garage door.

"I'm just trying to explain things."

Jeremy picked up his helmet. "I don't need any explanation."

"There's nothing to be scared of, you know. He's out of the picture."

"I'm not scared." Jeremy's eyes glanced at the house.

She looked where he was looking and appeared confused when she didn't see anything. "The thing is, I came here because I wanted to thank you. It sounds all cheesy and stuff, I know, but what you did was brave. It took a lot of courage to stand up to Kevin like that."

"I didn't know who he was." He climbed onto his scooter, keeping his eyes down. He worried if he looked directly at her, he'd forget about keeping his distance; the warning flares would be ignored.

"So you're saying, if you knew who he was you wouldn't have stepped in like that?"

He looked up. "You said that. Not me."

She smiled. "Have an extra helmet?"

He checked his phone. "I have to be to work soon."

"Yeah? Where are you working?" she asked.

"Danny's."

"I'm always in there. I haven't seen you," she said.

"I work in back."

"Are you cooking with Barry?"

He sighed and for some reason, felt embarrassed. "I wash dishes."

"Awesome. Barry's a good guy. I work just down the street from you. Paparazzi Cafe? My parents own the place. Have you been in there yet?"

Jeremy realized he'd not spent any time in town since returning home other than going to work. He shook his head.

"You'll have to come by. It's all done up with celebrity memorabilia. My dad is more than a movie buff; he's a freak about films."

"Maybe I will sometime," Jeremy said. He'd been in a hospital. It didn't mean he had been cut off from the rest of the world. He completed high school, watched TV and movies, read books and went on day trips. Still, he couldn't explain the way he felt if asked. His stomach was twisted into a knot and the palms of his hands were sweaty. Now that he had made eye contact with Greta, it became increasingly more difficult to look away. And she kept smiling at him. He would not allow himself to like this girl. Not a chance.

"Good." Greta looked down the driveway. "You have to go and I suppose I better get home. It's a long walk. And I don't want to waste my only day off."

Jeremy sighed, again. Against better judgment, he held out his helmet.

She cocked her head slightly to the side and offered up a half-smile. "You offering me a ride home?"

"You live far?"

She laughed. "I'm actually your closest neighbor."

* * *

Barry was leaning his back against the dumpster smoking a cigarette when Jeremy pulled into the parking lot.

"I'm sorry I'm late." Jeremy switched off his scooter and removed his helmet.

Barry looked him over. "Where have you been?"

Jeremy climbed off the scooter, set the helmet on the seat and said, "I had to give someone a ride home."

"A girl?"

Jeremy had exchanged phone numbers with Greta. He'd never called a girl before. One had never called him. The idea of talking with her on the phone left him discombobulated. He nodded.

Barry dropped his cigarette, crushed the lit end with his heel and smiled. "You're not late, kid. See you inside."

Jeremy breathed a sigh of relief.

Chapter 15

Jeremy thought his shift would never end. Stepping outside after Barry locked up, he took a moment and stared up at a bright moon in a black sky.

"Don't see stars like that living in the city. Too many lights interfere," Barry said. "You did real good tonight. Kept on top of things."

"Thank you."

Barry just nodded, fidgeting with the keys in his hand. "I'll see you tomorrow, then."

"See you tomorrow." Jeremy climbed onto his scooter. As was becoming usual, he waited for Barry to leave the back parking lot first before pulling out and onto the street.

Greta had sent him a few text messages earlier. He'd read them when he had the chance, but hadn't responded. He wasn't sure how to respond. She thanked him for the ride home. She offered him a free coffee and dessert if he ever stopped by the cafe. She wondered what he was up to tonight.

The car behind him was too close.

It took a moment before he recognized the car.

It was late. He had no idea what Kevin O'Sullivan was up to and neither was he interested in finding out. He pulled to the side of the road and waved the vehicle past.

Kevin pulled the car over, as well.

No one got out of the car. The driver hit the high beams. With the headlights shining on him, Jeremy couldn't see inside the windshield. The two of them just sat there. "This is crazy," he said out loud.

Jeremey started toward home, again.

The car followed with high beams on. The light hit Jeremy's side mirrors. It didn't distract him from the road in front of him, but he kept checking the mirrors. He didn't chance looking behind. He worried he might swerve. It felt as if the fender was close to hitting his rear tire. Bracing, he expected to be knocked off the scooter at any moment.

When he turned onto the next street, off the main road, the car pursued, sped past him and then cut across blocking the lanes. The driver door opened. Kevin climbed out of the car as Jeremy stopped several feet away from the car.

Jeremy kept his grip on the handlebars. Kevin's car blocked the two lanes but not the sidewalks. Jeremy wasn't boxed in by any means. The scooter had some *umph*. He imagined Kevin could pull him off the scooter if he tried going around the car.

"Where are you going?" Kevin folded his arms and leaned back against the side fender, leg up, knee bent, foot on the tire.

It felt rhetorical. Kevin was looking for a fight. Anything Jeremy said would set the kid off. Jeremy slowly backed the scooter up and turned the handlebars. Better to head back onto Main Street. Kevin was less likely to harass him there. He'd call his uncle for a ride.

He heard footfalls behind him and gunned the throttle.

As the scooter shot forward, a hand clasped onto the back of his sweaty t-shirt. Yanked back, he fell hard on the pavement. His tailbone sent waves of pain up his back and down his legs. He rolled onto his side and arched out hoping the sharp ache would subside.

"You're not going anywhere." Kevin stood over him. He grinned down at Jeremy.

Jeremy saw his scooter a few yards away. He hoped there was no permanent damage. He forced himself to stand, brushed his pants off. Without a word, he walked toward his scooter.

Kevin laughed. "Really? You're that big of a wuss. I knock you off your moped and you just take it?"

Jeremy ignored the taunt. He lifted his scooter. He couldn't see anything immediately wrong.

"This ain't over."

Jeremy sat on the seat.

Kevin jumped in front of the scooter, straddled the front tire and grabbed onto the handlebars.

"Just let me go," he said.

Kevin mimicked him. "*Just let me go!* Not a chance. I heard you were out with Greta earlier. Yeah. She told me all about it. We were laughing at you. You giving her a ride home like this is some kind of Harley or something. She was telling me how pathetic and crazy you were."

Frustration was nothing new. Jeremy lived his life drowning in the emotion. In the hospital, when allowed, he'd disappear into his room, climb into bed and hide. Dr. Burkhart suggested alternative ways for dealing with frustration. He wanted him to list his accomplishments, exercise, or spend time with supportive people. Hiding under the covers was generally more satisfying, but he never shared that truth with the doctor. "Why don't you leave me alone?"

The punch was unexpected. Kevin's fist came up and smashed him under the jaw. He bit his tongue. The blow knocked him off the scooter. The bike fell onto his leg. The heat from a hot engine scorched his leg through his jeans. He kicked at the scooter with his free foot and scooched backward, freeing his trapped leg.

He smelled burnt jeans, hair and flesh.

"Why don't you leave Greta alone? You asked for this. Thing is, you can't do anything about it. You're the crazy one. I know it. My father knows it. The town knows it. No one wants you here. The rumor is you were responsible for the death of your parents. There was even suspicion it was you who killed them. Fort Keeps doesn't need a whack-job around. My best advice? Go back to the psych-ward. Get out of this town. Leave these mountains." Kevin reared back and kicked Jeremy in the face.

Jeremy's head slammed back, the helmet bounced on the pavement. A siren sounded. Lights flashed.

Jeremy ran his hand under his nose, wiping away blood.

"What's going on here?" Sheriff O'Sullivan got out of his patrol car.

"Guy wiped out. I pulled over to see if he needed help," Kevin said, offering a hand to lift Jeremy up.

Jeremy moved away from him and sat up.

"You been drinking?" the sheriff asked.

"No, sir." Jeremy put both hands on the knee above his injured leg. The jeans were ruined. He wasn't bleeding, but his skin was blistered.

"We're going to have to give you a sobriety test." The sheriff lifted the scooter and set it up on the stand.

Who was the we? Jeremy got to his feet. "I just got out of work."

"Taking an attitude with me?"

"No, sir."

"Are you refusing the test?"

"No, sir."

Kevin laughed. "No, sir," he said, mocking Jeremy.

"That'll be all, Kevin. Head on home."

"But, dad—"

"Home, Kevin. Now."

Jeremy watched Kevin get back into his car. He gunned the engine. The tires spun, smoke rose from the pavement and then he sped away.

"How much have you had to drink?"

Jeremy took off his helmet. "Nothing."

"What caused the accident?" The sheriff walked back to his car. "Come over here."

Jeremy limped toward the O'Sullivan.

"You need an ambulance?"

Jeremy thought he might. He didn't want to delay getting home. He could treat the burns and bruises on his own. All he wanted was away from the sheriff. "I'll be fine."

"Take a deep breath and blow into this." He held up a rectangular device with a tube on the end.

"I haven't been drinking."

"Then there's nothing to worry about, is there?" O'Sullivan shoved the nozzle in Jeremy's face. "Blow."

Jeremy complied. The machine beeped.

Sheriff O'Sullivan's brow wrinkled and he frowned. "I'm going to ticket you for disorderly conduct. And I want you to head back to your uncle's place."

"Disorderly conduct? I didn't do anything?"

"Lower your voice!" The sheriff pointed at the buildings around them. "We've received enough complaints tonight about you racing up and down the streets. It's no wonder you didn't kill yourself. That might just be a glorified bicycle, but it has an engine. That makes it dangerous to you and to others. If you're not more careful, I'll have the damned thing impounded."

Jeremy ground his teeth. He kept his mouth shut.

"You have something you want to say?"

Jeremy lowered his eyes.

"That's better." He sat in the front seat of his car, kept the door open and wrote out the ticket. He tore off sheets of paper from his pad and handed them over to Jeremy.

"This is two tickets. One for not wearing a helmet. I was wearing my helmet."

"I don't recall seeing it on when I came upon you."

"I just took it off!"

"Listen here. You've been in town, what? A week? This is our second run-in already. I'm not sure how you managed to get out of St. Mary's, but I can tell you here, in my town, I don't tolerate troublemakers."

Jeremy stuffed the tickets in his pocket. "Can I go?"

O'Sullivan shook his head. "You know what? You'd better."

Chapter 16

Jeremy listened for the sound of the front door closing and then for the sound of Jack's truck pulling away.

He called work. A knot in his stomach twisted.

"Danny's."

It wasn't Barry. "Marsha?"

"Yeah?"

"It's Jeremy." He stared out the back window.

"Yeah, hon?"

Someone hid behind the trees. He pressed his nose against the glass. It had been a person.

"Jeremy?"

"I'm sorry, yes. I can't come in today. I feel sick." He moved his head this way and that, but couldn't get a better look. They were behind a tree at the edge of the property. He was sure of it.

"Barry's not here yet."

He didn't want to talk to the boss. "Could you tell him for me? I'm going right back to bed."

Jeremy imagined her shaking her head.

His face was swollen, lip split. Jack had been in bed when he got home last night. Dinner was wrapped and left for him in the microwave. He brought it to his room, just in case Jack came down while he was eating. "Please?"

"Sure, hon. You feel better." Marsha didn't sound convinced, but he was thankful she didn't give him a hard time.

"Thank you, I'll try." He ended the call and left his room.

He went outside through the front door, avoiding the back door in the kitchen. The air was crisp, cool. The grey sky promised rain. He should have grabbed a jacket. Instead, he hugged himself as we rounded a corner of the house.

Once in the backyard, Jeremy scanned the tree-line. He watched for any movement at all. He stood, waiting.

When nothing—no one—moved, he started toward the tree he'd seen the person lurking behind.

Dew covered the grass. The moisture wet through his sneakers. His socks and feet felt cold and damp.

He heard a noise. A branch snapped.

"I saw you, you know? From my window. I saw you." Jeremy stopped walking, waited. Overhead a hawk *screeched*. Jeremy didn't blink. He hoped he sounded brave. "Come out from back there!"

He was ready to run. If something popped out at him, he was out of there.

Ground crunched.

Someone stepped out from behind the tree.

"Greta," he whispered.

"What happened to your face?" She stood with hands clasped together in front of her. Part of her left arm and leg were still hidden behind the tree.

She shouldn't be here. Why was she sneaking around? Jeremy checked over his shoulder. He thought it might be an ambush. Kevin told him they'd laughed at him. "What are you doing here?"

"Want the truth? Or should I lie?"

He wasn't in a mood for games. "You should go."

She walked toward him. Every impulse told him to run, not look back. He stayed still, stayed where he was.

"What happened to your face?"

"I fell off the scooter."

She gasped. "Were you wearing your helmet? Are you okay?"

"Why were you hiding behind the trees?"

"You didn't answer any of my texts. I was worried."

He wasn't buying it. "Just looking for more things so you and Kevin can laugh at me?"

She stopped. "Laugh at you? What does Kevin have to do with anything?"

"Why aren't you at work?"

"I have the day off." She was only a few feet away. She raised an arm. Her finger traced the air in front of his face. "Does it hurt?"

"I told you, I'm fine." It was a trap. Kevin must be lurking around somewhere close by, watching, waiting.

"What are you looking for?"

"Where is he?"

Greta's brow furrowed. She turned around. "Where is *who*?"

"Kevin."

"We're not together anymore. I told you that already," she said. She almost touched him. "Did he do this?"

He leaned back, as if her hand were fire. "I had an accident."

"That bastard!"

"Forget it. He told me everything."

"*Everything* about what?"

He didn't want to repeat any of it, the thought alone was too humiliating. "I have to get back inside. I called in sick. I don't want to get caught out here."

"You called in sick? Are you?"

He wasn't. "I couldn't go in today."

"Because of the black eye and stuff?"

It wasn't black when he went to bed. Great. He'd never be able to hide that from his uncle.

"This is great."

"That I called in sick?" he asked.

"I'm off today, too."

"I can't do anything. If I'm seen out, my boss is going to know I'm not really sick."

"You think Barry's going to come check on you, see if you lied or not?" She laughed. "So what are you going to do all day, lay in bed in case Barry comes to the door?"

Jeremy looked back at the house, up at his bedroom window and shuddered. "I'd rather not."

"Wait, what is it?"

He shook his head, looked back at his window one more time. Was someone inside the house? Had Kevin slipped into the house while Greta was out here distracting him? "What are you up to?"

Greta's lips pursed. "I'm not up to anything."

"He's in the house, isn't he?" Jeremy turned away and ran around to the front of the house.

"Are you limping?" Greta was close behind him.

Ignoring her, he raced into the house and up the stairs.

"Who's up there?" Greta followed. "Who did you see?"

Jeremy threw open his bedroom door. He braced himself for a fight. Kevin had nerve breaking into his house.

The room was empty.

He stood in the doorway, panting. "He's not here."

"Who?"

"Kevin."

"Why would Kevin be here? Oh, you play guitar?" Greta pushed past him. She placed the guitar case on the bed. "Play me a song?"

"I'm going to ask you nicely to leave."

Greta stood up straight. Her facial expression drooped. "I don't know what Kevin told you."

"He said you guys were laughing at me." He hated admitting that.

"It's not true. I haven't spoken to him since that night you saw us fighting. He's called me a thousand times. I couldn't tell you how many texts he sent. But I haven't talked to him. Swear." She held up two fingers.

"What does that mean, the fingers?"

"It's a scout-thing."

"You were a scout?"

"No." She wrinkled her face up. "Were you?"

I grew up in a hospital, he thought. "No."

Greta turned around in the room. "So I have a question."

Jeremy didn't like that she'd grabbed his guitar. "What?"

"Who did you see inside the house?"

Jeremy saw his breath, it plumed in front of his face and dissipated. He shivered and hugged himself. "Nothing, no one."

"You saw something. You thought it was Kevin. Who else lives here?"

"Just me and my uncle," he said.

"I saw him leave already. So no one else should be inside the house." She squirmed and ran her hands up her arms. "Wow. I just got a chill."

"Let's go outside."

"It's going to rain," she said.

"We can't stay in here." Jeremy held open the bedroom door.

Greta didn't budge. "This is kind of weird."

"What is?"

"The way you're acting. It's like you're scared of something in the room."

Jeremy kept quiet.

"I don't believe it. You are. You're scared." She looked thrilled. Her grin was wide. White teeth were visible. You've seen the ghost, haven't you?"

His jaw must have dropped open.

Greta backed herself up against the wall. "Is she here? Can you see her?"

"Stop it." How could she know? Had she seen something, too? The last thing he wanted was to ask. What if he didn't like the answer? "That's crazy."

"Is she with us right now?" Greta ignored his ruse. Her eyes scanned the room, roving over the ceiling and closely inspecting the corners.

Jeremy went toward her. "I want you out of my room, out of this house, please."

"I have always heard the stories, I just never believed them."

"I'm not joking around, please." The room became very cold. He thought the windows frosted. He continued seeing his breath. Greta hadn't mentioned anything, though. And he couldn't see her breath.

Could he be imagining it, everything?

They'd spent countless therapy sessions discussing reality and fantasy, both in group and one-on-one with Dr. Burkhart.

He knew what was real. He knew what wasn't.

"Jeremy," Greta said. Her eyes opened wider. She had her hands pressed together under her chin. "Jeremy."

The door behind Jeremy slammed closed.

Greta screamed.

Chapter 17

Fort Keeps, NY — Adirondacks — October 1912

Sheriff Benji O'Sullivan rode his horse back to the spot where the Crosby girl's body was discovered. He knew who Alice was, and he also knew that she, like her mother in the day, was very attractive. Lots of boys forgot what they were doing whenever the girl walked by them. Beauty was often times as much a curse as it was considered a blessing, he supposed.

There would be doors to knock on. That could wait. The night was nearly over. The sun would be up soon. Despite the coffee he had at Dr. Marr's, his bones felt eternally cold. It wasn't just because of this murder, for a while now he'd felt an insistent cold inside he could never seem to warm.

Absent any moonlight, it was darker now. O'Sullivan wasn't worried about finding the spot where the body was recovered. They'd secured ribbons around the four corner trees marking the spot. Dismounting, he walked the mare over and slapped the reins around a tree.

He stood on the outside of the box and stared at matted grass.

A murder in Fort Keeps. Good Lord.

* * *

As the sun rose in front of him, O'Sullivan rode on his mare across the Gregory land. It was hilly, covered in trees and rocks. The sheriff was in no hurry. Confrontation came with the badge. O'Sullivan didn't look forward to talking with Mr. Gregory. There were few times when he could recall disliking his job. Today was one of them.

The log cabin had been in the Gregory family for a few generations. The wood fence outlined a postage-stamp portion of the property. O'Sullivan secured his horse to a post and, reluctantly, climbed the steps onto the front porch and knocked on the door.

Taking a step back, the sheriff hooked thumbs in his gun belt and waited.

Just as he thought about knocking a second time, the door opened.

"Mrs. Gregory, I hate to bother you at this hour," he said.

She was in an ankle length nightgown. She clutched the front in a hand, as if exposed otherwise. He saw the look in her eyes. The law at your door with the rising sun could only mean trouble. It was like her eyes scanned the ground searching for the reason for his visit. "Sheriff?"

"Is Mr. Gregory home?"

She looked behind her. It was an absent movement. "Is something the matter?"

"I'd prefer to speak with your husband."

She pulled open the door. "Would you like to come in?"

He thought about a warm house. He wanted nothing more than to get out of the dampness of the autumn morning. "I'll wait out here, ma'am. If you could get him for me, it would be appreciated."

She nodded, unable to hide the look of confusion in her wrinkled brow as she slowly closed the door on the sheriff.

Benji O'Sullivan stepped off the porch and walked across grass toward the wood fence. He placed a booted foot on the bottom rail, between posts. Staring up at the sky he watched the black sky surrender to soft blue and white scattered clouds.

A moment later he heard the front door open again, a creaking from old hinges giving away the action.

"Sheriff?"

O'Sullivan didn't relish turning, but sucked in a deep breath and as he exhaled, he rotated around. The man walking toward him was tucking his flannel shirt into the waistband of his trousers and working the buttons covering up dingy long-johns. He ran a hand under his chin, stroking a few days growth and eyed the sheriff with narrowed eyes.

"Mr. Gregory." O'Sullivan held out a hand. They shook. "I hate to bother you this early in the day."

"I was up. Just fixing to have breakfast. Wife's frying up some bacon and eggs. More than welcome to join us." It was a generous, but less than sincere, offer.

O'Sullivan said, "Thank you, sir. I'm going to have to pass."

"I see you've wasted no time getting to work this morning."

Been at it all night, he thought.

"What is it we can do for you? Got the missus all kinds of spooked right now, said you wouldn't explain to her what was going on." He struggled with getting his shirt tucked just right, adjusting himself this way and that.

"Thing is, I didn't want to upset her."

"She's plenty upset now. What is it sheriff? What possible reason could you have for coming out to my place at sunup?"

Sheriff Benji O'Sullivan squared his shoulders, and his jaw set. "Mr. Gregory, where were your boys last night?"

Chapter 18

"We're trapped!" Greta had her hands on Jeremy's back.

Jeremy held a protective arm out, keeping Greta behind him. His knees bent and leaning forward, he took a tentative step toward the door.

"What are you doing?"

"We can't just stand here," he answered. Her question rattled his nerve. His feet felt welded to the floor. He could hear only the both of them breathing. He sensed, however, someone else in the room with them. Something else. "Stay close."

She re-gripped a hold on his shirt. He felt fingernails scratch his back.

He stepped forward. Stopped.

The room was cold. The temperature dropping. The hairs inside his nostrils hardened. Greta whimpered. She was losing it. He felt her trembling, or it was him that shook.

The lights in the room came on.

A blackened figure stood in front of them, featureless, guarding the door.

"Leave us alone!" Jeremy's voice cracked, losing any sense of authority. He stood up straight, insulating Greta from any harm. "Get out of here!"

"Where is she?" The question was spat with a high-pitched and gravely cackle. The entity then exploded into beads as if black water sprayed from the end of a hose.

Jeremy screamed, throwing up an arm shielding himself from the spray.

The light stayed on.

The door opened, hinge whining in protest.

Jeremy fumbled for Greta's hand. "Come on!"

They ran out of the room. It felt like he couldn't move fast enough. He pushed Greta in front of him as they reached the stairs, certain whatever had been in his room was still behind them. He expected hands on his shoulders pulling him off his feet.

He stumbled on the first few stairs, the anticipation of an unknown attack stealing his balance.

"Jeremy!" Greta reached the bottom of the staircase, held out a hand for a grab hold. She hoisted Jeremy back onto his feet.

Ignoring the shooting pain in his tailbone, Jeremy followed Greta as they raced out of the house and into the cool air.

They didn't stop running until they traced the driveway and followed the declining slope down to the main road. Panting, they risked a look back.

"Are you okay?" Jeremy propped hands on hips and leaned back, catching his breath. He couldn't take his eyes off the front of the house. Even from this distance, he expected to see the front door open.

If the door opened, would he see the ghost exit? The thought alone was enough that he blinked hard and turned away. He didn't want to witness anything paranormal. There was only one good thing coming out of everything that just happened. He knew he wasn't crazy. Crazier. "You saw that, right?"

Greta's eyes were opened wide.

"Greta. You saw that. Tell me you saw that?" He pointed toward the house. His shirt stuck to his skin. The sweat was chilling, becoming cold. An icy shiver ran up his spine.

"I don't know what I saw." She shook her head, as if trying a desperate attempt at removing everything from her memory.

He did not want to hear that. Her witness was essential. No one would ever believe him. Jeremy had no intention of telling a soul. Still, if it came down to it, he could and Greta could back up his testimony.

"The door closing. Opening. The lights. The figure, the woman—she exploded!"

His words appeared to push her into a fit. Backing away from him, that head still shaking, she said, "No. I saw the door close. The darkness. I can't remember ever being in a room so dark."

"And the figure, the woman—"

"I didn't see anything."

"She was in front of us. Blocking the door, keeping us from escaping." How could she have not seen the apparition?

"I was behind you the whole time. I heard noises and it was so dark."

It had been dark. The absence of light didn't keep him from seeing whatever it was he saw.

"I had my eyes closed. I just closed my eyes tight. I've never been that scared."

She closed her eyes? Jeremy felt deflated. His shoulders sagged.

"What are you going to do?" she asked.

"What do you mean?" At least she was standing still, now. No longer backing away from him, away from the house. She folded her arms. He couldn't tell if she hugged herself for comfort, or if it was because she was cold.

"The house. You can't go back in there."

"I live there." He thought about his uncle. Had Jack seen anything? He'd been staying at the house for years. "I have to go back."

"I don't think that's such a good idea."

"It's my home." Was this going to shatter their friendship?

Were they friends?

"You knew there was a ghost," he said. He had to find out. He might not care for the response, but for some reason she wasn't surprised the place might be haunted.

"It's nothing, a legend." She looked down at the loose gravel as the toe of her shoe moved stones out in an arc. "At least that's what I always thought."

"What is?"

"The Woman in the Woods. That's what everyone has always called it," she said, now watching him. "You haven't heard the story? There are so many variations. They all kind of start the same. Took place back in the nineteen hundreds. This woman's daughter goes missing and when they find the body, either the girl has been raped and murdered, or murdered, or they never find the body. Doesn't really matter. Point is, the mother doesn't take the news well. She goes insane. Some say she sought revenge against those involved and then killed herself and others say she just killed herself. Anytime I have heard it told, she always kills herself. From the day of her death until now," Greta pointed at the house, "people claim to have seen her in the woods. It's said she roams the area looking to protect young girls from boys."

Jeremy rubbed his hand over goosebumps on his arm. He'd never seen anything in the woods. "That's got nothing to do with my house."

"It's got everything to do with your house." Greta, again took steps away from him, away from the driveway. She stood in wet grass, hands stuffed into pockets. "That's where they say the family lived, the mother and her daughter. It was different then, a ranch house. Didn't have the upstairs like it does now."

Jeremy had questions. "The mother *killed* herself in the house?"

Greta shrugged. "Depends who retells the story. In the house, in the woods, with a gun, hung from a noose."

Jeremy looked at the house. His thoughts jumbled. "It's just a legend."

Greta humphed. "Yeah, just a legend. I mean, I never thought there was anything to it."

Until now, Jeremy thought.

* * *

Jeremy opened his eyes. He was on his stomach; lying on the sofa in the front family room. He didn't remember falling asleep. When had he come back into the house? Where was Greta?

He blinked once. Twice.

Seated in the chair across from him was a girl. Her feet were up on the cushion and thin, pasty white almost green skinned arms were wrapped around her legs. Long, wet looking black hair covered her face and yet he was certain she watched him. Had she been staring at him while he slept?

Jeremy felt an undefined weight press down on his back. It kept him from jumping up and running away. His ribs ached and his breathing became labored. He wasn't sure what held him down. He couldn't move his head, either. He felt paralyzed.

Who are you? No sound escaped his lips. He wasn't sure his mouth even moved. If it had, if he had spoken, then he couldn't hear himself.

A loud, solid thud came from upstairs.

His ears worked.

The head of the girl in the chair pivoted toward the sound. It was as if something heavy like a bowling ball dropped onto hardwood floors. He didn't think there was a bowling ball upstairs. Maybe it was Uncle Jack's?

He couldn't look away from her.

Slowly, she rotated her head back toward him. Thankful he couldn't see her eyes, he understood why Greta had shut hers earlier. He wanted his closed, but couldn't.

No muscle in his body responded to his wishes.

Who are you?

Nothing. No sound. No words.

No answer.

His eyes opened, again.

He was in the family room. On the sofa. He pushed up, kneeling on the cushions. Looking around, the room was dark.

The chair where he had seen the girl was not by the sofa.

It was in a corner of the room.

Empty.

He heard a loud thud come from upstairs.

Chapter 19

It was the aroma of bacon that brought him around. The sound of something sizzling in a frying pan had him sniffing the air before opening his eyes.

"Hungry?"

Uncle Jack wore an apron around his waist. Hand smears on the front looked so old it would be easy to assume they were thinking them part of the fabric.

"Is it morning?" Jeremy heard himself speak this time. It was a wonderful sound.

"I heard you'd called in sick to work yesterday. When I got home, you were sound asleep. I thought about waking you, having you go up to your room. I figured why wake you up to tell you to go to sleep?"

Jeremy sat up on an arm.

He was on the sofa. In the family room. The chair where the girl sat in the corner. Empty. Only this time he knew he was awake. There was no doubt.

"What happened?"

"What happened to what?" Jeremy rubbed his eyes. His mouth was dry. He ran his tongue around the roof of his mouth and across a buildup of film on the back of his teeth.

"Your face."

The bruising. It must look ten times worse today. Jeremy sat up, but looked down. "I fell off the moped the other night."

"Weren't you wearing your helmet?" The concern in his tone of voice was evident, despite the accusatory words chosen. He softened then. "Are you alright?"

Jeremy wanted to tell his uncle what was going on. The sheriff and his son had it in for him. How did you fight the law? What stopped him from talking was fear. If Uncle Jack said anything, who knew what kind of trouble the sheriff would start. Jack didn't need the hassle. He'd already done so much. "I'm fine. Banged up a little."

"And the moped?"

"It's okay. In the garage."

"Well, you still don't look so good. On my way into work, I'm going to stop in and talk to your boss. You just rest."

"I can go back to work today," Jeremy said. It was because he didn't want to go back, that he knew he should. The longer he stayed home, the harder it would become to return.

Then there was the house. He didn't want to spend another day inside the house. He couldn't imagine being left alone. Not today. Not after what happened yesterday.

Where was Greta?

Why couldn't he remember saying goodbye to her last night?

"You don't have to do that," Jeremy said.

"Are you sure? Nothing wrong with taking another day off." The way he said it made it sound as if he'd been skeptical about him having called in the day before. The black eye, swollen nose and split lip must have convinced him otherwise.

He and Greta had been standing at the end of the driveway by the main road. He didn't remember a single car passing. He couldn't recall saying goodbye.

That bothered him.

He couldn't recall walking back up to the house, going into the house, or falling asleep on the sofa.

But he couldn't recall saying goodbye to Greta.

He thought if he had, he'd have watched her walk away. In fact he knew he would have watched her until he couldn't see her walking anymore. And even then he imagined he'd have stayed where he was just staring at where she had been.

He liked her. There was no way around it. Despite Kevin's beating and his father's threats, he couldn't just force his heart to surrender. It wasn't that easy. Admitting she occupied his mind more and more wasn't dangerous. Acting on those feelings, on the other hand, was a different story.

She must have felt something, too. Why else would she have hidden behind a tree in his backyard? Sure, that was kind of creepy, a little stalker-*ish*. He didn't look at it that way. It was just the opposite, actually. He was flattered. If anything, she had saved him the humiliating task of searching for the perfect way to force a spontaneous conversation.

"Jer? Are you okay?"

He realized he had his eyes closed tight. The focus was on remembering. He knew if he could call to mind a memory of saying goodbye to Greta... "Just a headache," Jeremy lied.

"Well, I think that settles it."

"Settles what?"

"Sit back. Let me fix you a plate of food. Watch some TV or something. I'm going to see Barry before I head into work."

"I think I should go in today."

"I know you do." Jack went into the kitchen. Jeremy heard the familiar sounds of food scrapped from a pan to a plate. "I respect that. I do. Shows good work ethic. Your daddy was like that. Hell. Suppose I am, too."

Jack came back into the room, he held a plate of scrambled eggs, crisp bacon and toast in one hand and a large glass of orange juice in the other. He set them down on the coffee table by the sofa. "That's why you don't have to feel bad about missing another day of work. It's not like you're faking it."

"But, Uncle Jack..."

"Eat up and then get a little more rest. I'll try to get out a little early tonight." He stepped into his boots by the door, left the laces loose and lifted his Carhartt brown coat off the hook on the back of the door.

"What if Barry fires me for missing two days of work?" Jeremy didn't enjoy washing dishes and scrubbing pots and pans. He needed the job, was thankful for it, even. He knew he wouldn't spend the rest of his life behind the kitchen. And yet...

"Barry isn't going to do any such thing. Seriously, forget about it. Get some rest. Let me handle this, okay?"

There was something comforting about having his uncle take control. It dispelled some of the growing anxiety he felt.

Jeremy lifted the plate and tried breakfast. "This is good."

"Don't talk with your mouth full." Jack winked. "We agreed?"

"Agreed."

When Jack left the house, Jeremy reached for the TV remote and switched on the television. Before forking more eggs into mouth, Jeremy froze.

In the glass reflection from the picture window over the television, he saw her.

The girl from his dream; the one who had been sitting in the chair. Only this time she stood in the archway between the living room and the kitchen.

She pointed toward the staircase.

Jeremy dropped the plate of food and leapt off the sofa. He stumbled, banging his shin against the coffee table and swiveled toward where he'd seen the girl, the ghost—whatever she was, it was!

No one was there.

A loud, solid thud came from upstairs.

"Not again," Jeremy said, "no, not again!"

Chapter 20

Fort Keeps, NY — Adirondacks — October 1912

Sheriff Benji O'Sullivan wore a long tan leather jacket that just reached the bottom of his calf muscles. His boots were scuffed beyond polishing and the soles worn nearly clean off. He'd need a new pair before winter. The idea of spending money on even essentials gave him pause. Only reason he considered the purchase was his overwhelming fear of frostbite and losing toes.

He stood outside his office. Cigar smoke plumed in front of his face. The crisp autumn air was refreshing, just invigorating enough that he felt alert. It had been a long night. He'd been awake nearly thirty hours. Wasn't often they had many big crimes in Fort Keeps. With all signs pointing toward a murder, he couldn't imagine going home and sleeping. Rest could wait. He had a mourning mother at home desperate for answers.

He also had a father waiting at the corner bar hoping his boys don't get arrested on murder charges, waiting for him to come down and deliver a verdict.

Resolution was not going to make everyone happy.

Nothing ever did.

He let the stogie extinguish naturally. He flicked away ash and placed the remaining cigar into a pocket for later.

Postponing the inevitable expired. It was time for the interrogation and he just wasn't looking forward to questioning two kids. The roiling in his gut didn't help matters. When all indications point in the same direction...

He sucked in a last lungful of fresh air and walked into his office before exhaling a long, slow sigh. He closed the door, shutting it with a little more force than was needed. The bang punctuated his return and brought about the desired effect.

The Gregory boys sat side by side in front of his desk. Jacob had been leaning back on the chair's two legs. He dropped forward and the grin he wore dissipated fast.

"You know why I brought you here?" O'Sullivan sat on the corner of his desk. The office housed by two cells in back. Iron bars and iron bars boxing cinder block walls. Rest of the place was simple log construction. Across from him was where his deputy sat. The desk a little smaller. He had no idea if it was intentional. Stature and all that.

"Our father didn't say." Caleb was the older of the two. Seventeen still made him a minor in New York.

"Is it something serious, sheriff?" Although Jacob was two years younger, he was a head taller. The boys packed on muscle. It wasn't like they farmed. He knew they spent a lot of time with their father swinging axes, taking down trees and splitting wood.

O'Sullivan stood up. He shrugged off his jacket and hung it on the hook behind the door. Part of everything he did was tactical. Planned. The idea was to make them sweat, get them a bit apprehensive. He wanted their imaginations running wild. People were more likely to spill information accidentally. Normally, he'd have separated the brothers, not let them have time to mesh stories. These two lived together. They had hours to work out details.

If, that was, they were guilty of anything.

His job was to assume guilt until proven innocent. Not the other way around. It troubled him that at the moment these were his only two and most likely suspects in the murder.

"Let me ask you this." O'Sullivan stood behind his desk, palms down and leaned toward them. Standing gave him authority and the leaning displayed his intimidating power. "Why do you think I've brought you down here today?"

Neither immediately answered. Jacob's eyes searched, briefly, for Caleb's reaction before going back to watch his hands folded in his lap.

"Caleb?"

No eye contact. "No, sir."

"Jacob?"

A slight shake of his head. "No, sir."

"I'd like to hear about what you boys did yesterday evening."

No one spoke. O'Sullivan let minutes pass and then he hammered a hand on the desk. Both Gregorys looked up, startled as if they'd drifted off to sleep and were awakened suddenly from a thunderclap. "Jacob! What were you up to last night?"

The kid might be the bigger of the two, but was still *just* fifteen. O'Sullivan wanted to whittle away at any confidence he might harbor.

"When?" Jacob said. It was quiet. Barely audible.

"When, what?" the sheriff asked.

"You asked us where we were last night. I just want to know if you have a specific time in mind."

O'Sullivan suddenly surmised he'd misjudged the youths. 'Tell you what. Stand up. Get up. Now!"

Jacob stood. He was nearly as tall as the sheriff. They stood toe to toe. O'Sullivan found it difficult remembering the guy in front of him was just a kid. "Come with me."

"Where we going?"

He'd handled it wrong from the start. Having the brothers together didn't help matters. It hindered them. Either Jacob was showing off in front of his big brother, or Caleb was the weaker link.

"A little tour of the facility." The sheriff grasped Jacob's forearm. "Follow me."

He took the kid toward the back, lifted the ring of keys from the hook and unlocked the door.

"After you." The sheriff motioned with a wave of his hand.

Jacob eyed him, unblinking, before walking through.

O'Sullivan turned his head. "You," he said, pointing at Caleb. "Sit tight. I'll be right back."

Closing the door behind them, O'Sullivan fought grinning. He thought he caught a flicker of fear pass over Jacob's otherwise calm and collected demeanor. Without a word, he walked past the boy, past the first cell and unlocked the gate into the second. The hinges squeaked as it swung open. The cells didn't get that much use. Weekend intoxicated regulars often slept off the alcohol in these confined spaces. "I am going to have you wait in here for a while."

Jacob didn't move. "Why's that?"

O'Sullivan knew he didn't need to explain himself. "I want to have a word with your brother."

"So why do I have to be locked up?"

"I have questions. I need answers. I want to see if you both give me the same answers. Only way I can make sure that happens is if when Caleb talks, you're not there to hear what's said."

"That's not what I meant."

The sheriff was beginning to dislike this boy. "What did you mean?"

"I'm not under arrest am I? As far as you know, I've done nothing wrong. Isn't that right?"

"It is."

"So why are you going to cage me like a criminal?"

O'Sullivan realized he'd been mistaken, again. It couldn't have been fear he saw in the boy. It must have been something else entirely. "Get in the cell."

Jacob wrinkled his nose and shrugged. His jaw set. "If that's what you want."

"It is." The sheriff locked the gate once Jacob was inside. "Make yourself comfortable. This might take a while."

Chapter 21

Work had become the most monotonous thing in his life. Scrubbing pots and pans and washing dishes kept his hands busy, but left his mind wide open. While he worked all he could do was think about things. That was maddening, in and of itself.

Before work, Jeremy had picked up medication refills at the pharmacy. When he rode his moped by the Paparazzi Cafe, he couldn't help looking over at the front glass windows where a constant succession of flashbulbs popped. The strobe light effect made seeing inside nearly impossible. The hope he'd catch a glimpse of Greta was dashed.

He remembered when stopped for the only red light in town, he'd chanced one last look back. He had that odd sensation of being watched and hoped Greta had seen him pass by the cafe and came out to look for him. That hadn't been the case. She wasn't standing by the door. He searched the area and didn't see anyone looking at him.

He knew he didn't really know her. Not well. Hardly at all.

He missed her, though.

The daily routine of working long hours and sleeping quickly became a bore. His days off didn't align with Uncle Jack's. He killed time playing guitar, but after a while even doing something he enjoyed dulled. He hated admitting it, but at least when he was living at the hospital he was surrounded by people. There was always someone to talk to there. Now he felt a little guilty about having spent most of his time *avoiding* those desperate for conversation.

He missed his room in the hospital.

The last several days he'd slept on the sofa in the family room. Uncle Jack questioned him about it. Many times he came close to sharing with his uncle the events that had unfolded, but stopped himself. Maybe he didn't miss his room and the exchange at the hospital, half as much as he thought.

Using his uncle's computer, he'd done some research on the a woman in the woods. Greta didn't know the half of it. There were countless renditions behind the legend. Some said the ghost of the mother roamed through the woods with two, large attack dogs on chain leashes. And when she caught a couple making out, she'd loose the dogs on the boy and yell for the girl to run.

The ghost story supposedly had truth behind it, though. Jeremy just couldn't figure out how to sort fact from fiction.

It had been some time since Allana or Marsha last brought in a filled bus tray. That was a good sign. The night was nearly over.

Jeremy did his best to not look at the time. It made the evening drag. It was the whole watching a pot of water boil thing. What hindered the regime was checking his phone for messages. Every now and then Jack texted him, letting him know what's for dinner, or if he was going to be out late, or something. Even though almost two weeks have passed since he last talked to Greta, he caught himself looking for new messages. There were never any from her.

What he did find, every time he pulled out his phone, was the time. Brightly displayed on the screen. *So* that *was the downside to feeling needy*, he determined.

When the door swung open, Jeremy was just finishing up the last of the pots. His stomach sank a little. He didn't want to turn around. Ready to go home, the last thing he wanted to see was another bus tray filled with dirty dishes, glasses and silverware.

"About ready, Jer?" Barry said.

Yes. "I am."

"I let the ladies go. I'm gonna run a mop over everything and we're out of here."

"I should be ready by then."

* * *

When Jeremy and Barry exited the back of the diner, Greta was standing by the moped.

"Hey," she said.

Barry's eyebrows arched and then he did his best to mask any expression. He turned to Jeremy. "Have a good night."

"Thanks."

"Good night, Greta."

"See ya, Barry."

Jeremy thought he heard his boss chuckle as he got into his vehicle and pulled out of the parking lot.

"How've you been?" Greta asked.

"Good. You?"

"Good."

"Getting cold out at night." Jeremy had no idea what else to say.

"Yeah."

They stood there.

"You just get out of work?" Jeremy asked.

"About an hour ago. I was thinking about heading over to Wood Fire for some pizza." She looked in the direction of the pizzeria.

"Oh. That sounds good. I haven't tried their pizza yet."

"It's good. The best, really."

He didn't know much about pizza. They served it in the cafeteria at St. Mary's. On some occasions when the floor celebrated something special, pizza was delivered from outside, actual pizza places. Cafeteria pizza was then inedible for the next few weeks. "I haven't had good pizza in a while."

"Did you wanna…"

"You inviting me?"

"Are you hungry?"

He wasn't. Not really. Barry fed him well throughout the shift. "I could eat," he said and patted his stomach. "But what I really need is a shower. I don't smell so good."

Greta laughed, as if he'd said something cute. "Don't be ridiculous. You're fine."

He wasn't. If anything, he now found himself more aware of his own odor. Chicken, macaroni and cheese and dead sweat. "Did you walk?"

"I did. From the cafe."

How would she have gotten home if he declined the offer? "Hop on?"

"Sure."

Jeremy remembered the last time he had given her a ride. He'd loved her close, hugging him. This time he cringed as she wrapped arms around his chest. He stunk and was so dirty and yet, she didn't seem the least bit fazed.

Jeremy parked in front of Wood Fire Pizzeria. It took all of fifteen seconds to get there from the diner. Greta had her arms wrapped around him the entire time. He wished they could keep going, would give most anything if the moment could last just a little longer.

Inside, the aromas filling the pizza shop made his mouth water. He smelled the sauce, cheese, doughy bread and Italian seasoning. There were a few booths along the side wall and tables between the counter.

"What do you like on your pizza?" Greta said.

"I'll just trust you."

Greta smiled and turned to face the woman by the register waiting to take their order. "Hiya, Samantha."

"How are you, Greta?"

"Starving! Have you met Jeremy Raines yet?"

Samantha looked about forty, brown hair pulled back in a ponytail. She wore a white visor with the name and logo of the pizzeria on it, which was also decaled onto her red t-shirt. "I haven't." She introduced herself. "Are you new in town?"

Jeremy shook her hand. "More or less."

"Wait a minute. Raines. Raines." She tapped a finger against her lip and then her eyes darted left and opened wider.

Jeremy knew Samantha remembered his past. "Greta said everything here is the best."

Samantha looked thankful for the comment. The subject changed. She was free and clear. "She eats here at least once a week. She better say that! What can I get for the two of you?"

"Trust me?" Greta asked Jeremy.

"Completely."

"Sam, can we have a medium Mediterranean and two sodas. Diet for me. Jeremy?"

"Full sugar, please."

"Medium Mediterranean, two drinks. Got it. Go have a seat. I'll bring it over when it's ready." Samantha tore the order off the pad, clipped it to a wheel and spun it around to the guys cooking in the back.

"Sit by a window?" Greta asked.

"Sure." They sat. He said, "Mediterranean pizza?"

"It's a white sauce, with mozzarella and feta cheese. They top it with spinach, roasted red peppers and sliced tomatoes."

"What's a white sauce?"

"Like an oil and garlic."

He thought about his breath. She'd be eating it, too. "Sounds ... different. Good, I mean. It sounds good, but different."

"What do you normally get on your pizza?"

"Pepperoni."

Samantha came over with the sodas. "Diet. And not diet."

They thanked her. When she was gone, Greta took a sip from the straw in her glass. "Okay. So I went down to the Inlet Library. I was looking into your house."

He was intrigued. Truth was, he thought he'd seen the last of her that day after the ghost trapped them in the house. Here she was, though, asking him out to eat and telling him she'd been doing research. "What did you find?"

"Quite a bit, actually. Okay. Are you ready for this? I found that a lady, Elissa Crosby, is the one who owned your house and the land around it, back in the very early nineteen hundreds. So I had the librarian show me how to search old copies of The Adirondack Herald using microfiche," she said.

"Microfiche? What's that?"

"I didn't know either. They used to take pictures of every page of a newspaper, or magazine and then stored thousands and thousands of editions on a rolled up piece of film. I had to use a machine where light passed through the negative and let me view the images on the monitor. If that makes sense?"

"Kind of." He had no idea what she was talking about.

"It wasn't easy. Not at first. But that's beside the point," she said. "I explained to the librarian what I was attempting and she was extremely helpful. She and I spent the last few days digging up information. Anyway, this old newspaper covered the murder of a young girl named, Alice Crosby."

"Same last name as the lady who owned my house."

"Right. It was October, 1912." She pushed her soda to the side. She had her arms on the table. "There were a few articles about this Alice. She was found in the woods. The crime was investigated by the sheriff." Greta rolled her eyes.

"What?"

"I knew Kevin's family has been here in the mountains forever, but I didn't realize his, like, great-great grandfather was also sheriff. Benji O'Sullivan was the sheriff back in 1912. He had a place deeper in the woods, higher up the mountain. Kevin and his dad still use the place when they go hunting."

Jeremy didn't want to ruin the night thinking about Kevin. "Wow, no kidding?"

"Dead honest." She craned her neck, sipped more soda. "Two brothers were charged with the murder. They were kids."

"And then what happened?"

Chapter 22

Fort Keeps, NY — Adirondacks — October 1912

Sheriff Benji O'Sullivan stepped out of the corner bar. He'd left a broken man inside. He explained that, for the time being Jacob and Caleb would remain in custody while things got sorted out. There wasn't much to sort out. Caleb broke down crying when questioned. No confession, but nearly as good as one. Jacob would be tougher. He had them separated. A deputy stayed with Caleb. O'Sullivan wanted Jacob isolated.

He wished he had news for Ms. Crosby. Regardless, he retrieved his horse from the post. A ride out to her place was in order. She'd been alone for the better part of a day. Mourning couldn't start for some, until a sense of justice was delivered. He couldn't give her that, but wanted her aware of some facts. Maybe a little bit of satisfaction could come from the fact suspects were in custody. Perhaps not. Either way, she had a right to know.

Her house looked the same tonight as it did last night when he first came calling with news they'd found a body, small, frail and insignificant. Alice would count on him for answers.

Someone sat in a rocking chair on the front porch.

The sheriff dismounted and led his mare by the reins. "Ma'am?"

The woman didn't move.

"Gonna get sick sitting out here without a coat on." O'Sullivan couldn't believe she was in nothing more than a white nightgown. She was in the same one she wore the night before.

He climbed the porch step, tentatively. A lantern burned bright on a small table beside Elissa. She hadn't so much as blinked in the time he'd been observing her. Wavy hair was loose and hung well past mid-chest. Bare feet rested flat on what had to be ice cold boards. Her arms lay on the rests, while limp hands dangled. "Ms. Crosby?"

Slowly, her head turned and tilted up toward the sound of his voice.

The whites of her eyes were crimson. Streaks made by cried tears cut through dried dirt covering most of her face.

Fresh tears brimmed along her bottom lids. Her lips quivered.

O'Sullivan took a knee beside her.

She dropped her head onto his shoulder. He wrapped an arm around her. "You're freezing. How long have you been out here? Come on. Let's get you inside. C'mon, now."

He rose, helping her to her feet. She stood, easy enough. With his guidance, she allowed herself to be walked inside. The sofa in front looked inviting enough. He set her down on it, retrieved blankets off the bed out of the closest room and then got to work on starting a fire in the hearth.

"Did you find who did it?"

O'Sullivan had been stoking the flames. "Ms. Crosby?"

"Did you find the one who hurt my daughter?"

Alice wasn't hurt. She was dead. There was a difference. She might be in denial, shock. It worried him. "We have two suspects in custody, ma'am. It's why I came out here tonight. I wanted to keep you—"

"Did you kill them?"

If O'Sullivan hadn't have been staring at her, he would have sworn the question came from somewhere else in the house. "Elissa—"

"Did you kill them?"

It was her. She said it. Her arms were on the outside of the blankets, hands balled into fists.

"I'm just the law, ma'am. They're locked away for now. No one has been arrested yet. They are suspects at this point. Nothing more."

Elissa sobbed. Her shoulders shook and her chin was against her chest. Her fingers never unrolled. "They don't deserve to live. Not after what they did to my daughter. Not after the way they hurt my little girl."

"Once we know for sure—"

"She hasn't stopped crying, not once since I got home."

O'Sullivan stood up. "Who hasn't?"

"Alice. Don't you hear her?" Elissa pointed toward the back of the house. "There's nothing I can do to help her. There's not a thing I can do to take away her pain. Listen to her calling out for me, 'Help me, Mom. Help me.'"

O'Sullivan stood still. He listened. There was nothing. The wood in the fire crackled. Snapped. Some of the smoke came back into the house. Was the flue opened?

He didn't expect to hear Alice.

Grieving was powerful. Elissa Crosby was alone now. It could be years before she felt any better, if getting used to her daughter having been murdered was even possible.

He didn't think it was.

"She's crying for me! There's nothing I can do and they're hurting her."

O'Sullivan sat on the couch beside Elissa. There weren't magic words. He couldn't imagine her loss. No parent should suffer the death of a child. There was an expectation he say something. "No one is hurting Alice anymore."

Her jaw set and she continued jabbing a finger toward the back of the house. "Then why is she crying?"

For just a moment, O'Sullivan thought he heard it, the crying coming from somewhere else inside the house.

A young girl crying.

He stood up, strained to hear, turning his head slightly to the side. Nothing.

It was his imagination, had to be. Elissa's hysteria was contagious. There was no one crying. Not a sound but the two of them breathing.

And yet, for several more seconds he stood as still as a deer in a field and listened.

Chapter 23

Samantha brought over pizza and carried two plates in her other hand. "One Mediterranean. Just out of the oven!"

Setting everything down, Samantha used the spatula under a thin crust and served up a triangle slice onto each plate. "There you have it. Anything else you need? No? Enjoy."

"Looks amazing." Jeremy lifted his slice. Cheese oozed back down to his plate. He finger twirled and tossed the cheese string back onto his piece.

"Tastes even better!" Greta folded her slice and bit in. She fanned a hand in front of her mouth. "Ooh. Hot."

Once they slowed down on eating, Greta leaned in across the table. "Can I ask you something? It's personal. And I fully understand if you don't want to talk about it. But rather than listening to rumors, I'd rather come to you directly, if that's okay?"

"It's okay."

"What happened? I mean, why were you away for so long?"

Jeremy looked at the table, noticed the polish over swirling wood. He could see a shadow of his reflection. Dark. Brooding.

She reached across the table. Her hand landed over his. "I'm sorry. That was rude. I had no business asking that."

"It's okay. I really don't mind telling you." He figured it was a lot like the legend of the Woman in the Woods. People who knew he was back, like Kevin, spread different tales about town. None had made it back to him. That wasn't surprising, though. More than anything, he at least wanted Greta to hear the truth, as he remembered it anyway, from him. "I was eight years old…"

* * *

Jeremy was in his room. He heard his parents arguing downstairs. Even at his age he knew something was wrong. Normally, Mom and Dad didn't even talk to each other. The raised voices scared him.

He ventured out into the hallway. The yelling was louder here. He tiptoed toward the stairs. They wouldn't have been able to hear him if he stomped his way down the hall. He just didn't want them catching him eavesdropping.

Halfway down the stairs, he stopped, squatted and pressed his face between guardrail slats.

"You, of all people," his father said. He'd stopped yelling. "I never saw it coming. I mean, I just never thought you would do this to me. To us. What about our family? What about Jeremy? Did you ever just stop and think about us for a minute?"

"It wasn't like that," his mother said.

"No?" He sounded a little more agitated. It was evident even in the way he said a two-letter word. "What was it like, Erica? Tell me. Because I wasn't there. What was it like?"

"Abe, don't. Let go of me. That hurts."

"I want to know, dear." The words seethed as if filled with venom. "Tell me."

"Let me go, Abe." His mother matched his tone, but her voice quivered. "We can talk about this. But not this way."

Jeremy moved down the stairs and at the bottom, he chanced a look around the banister. He saw his father's back. His mother looked like she might be pressed against the counter.

He wanted the fighting to stop.

His father raised a hand, high over his head.

Jeremy wished they'd just quit yelling.

His father swung.

Pressing his hands over his ears, Jeremy opened his mouth to scream.

He heard the smack. His mother tumbled backward, out of view. His father fumbled both hands toward her.

She fell.

He saw her legs on the floor.

Jeremy couldn't remember if he'd actually screamed. He might have. His father never looked his way. So maybe he didn't.

"No. Get up, Erica. Don't mess around." His father took a knee. Jeremy saw him lean over his mother. It looked as if he shook her by the shoulders.

Jeremy moved in closer. He stayed by the wall. Getting caught spying would get him punished. There was no way he was staying in this weekend. Everyone was going fishing. He had new lures he couldn't wait to test.

His stomach felt heavy. Despite the weightiness it flipped and flopped. He put a hand over his belly button and pressed hard. That did absolutely nothing to relieve the queasy sensation.

His father was crying. There was not a single time he could recall when he'd witness his father cry.

His own eyes watered.

"Wake up, Erica. Get up."

His Mom. Something was wrong.

The setting sun shone directly into the kitchen. Bright. Blinding. Jeremy risked another step closer. He was far from the safety of the stairs. He did his best to blend and remain invisible.

The back door opened...

* * *

Jeremy sat back in the booth at the pizzeria and sucked in a deep breath.

"Jeremy? What is it?"

He remembered something. It was the first time. In all the years he talked to his doctor, in group, he never recalled having seen the back door open.

The realization had pulled him out of the rendition.

"We should get going," Jeremy pushed his plate away.

"Are you alright?" Greta slid over in the booth, moving closer to Jeremy.

Every muscle in his body tensed, knotted. His fingers curled, as if he had the hands of a witch with gnarled and knobby knuckles. His breathing became irregular. He huffed, unable to fill his lungs. He pushed himself out of the booth. "I can give you a ride home, but we have to go now."

He didn't know why he was so anxious.

The new memory had him unraveling.

Peripherally, he saw Samantha watching him.

Greta stared at him, her lips parted, eyes wide. "We should sit for a minute. Give you a chance to calm down."

Inside his head he tried counting from one to ten.

He couldn't get past three. His clothing felt restricting. Tugging at his collar didn't relieve pressure. Tracing fingers up and down his arms did nothing to steady the shaking.

"You know what?" Samantha said. "If you gotta run, I can see to it that Greta gets home safely. Nothing for you to worry about."

She was afraid of him. Her stance was a tell. She looked ready to clobber him with the rolling pin covered in flour, casually dangling from her right hand.

"Is that okay with you?" Jeremy looked Greta in the eyes. He'd have looked into those eyes all night if she would have let him.

If things hadn't suddenly soured.

"Ah, yeah. Yes. That's fine." Was she scared of him, too?

Of course they were. *You're acting like a freak!* He thought. His hands tugged at his hair and then patted it down.

It was better this way. Jeremy was convinced they'd never see each other again after the way he acted tonight. He couldn't blame her.

Backing up, away from the booth and toward the door, he tried waving.

It looked foolish. He lowered his arm. "Thank you," he said. "The pizza was great."

"Glad you enjoyed it." Samantha stepped further into her own dining area, was headed toward Greta. The protective movements were not lost on Jeremy. It was clear if he made any sudden move back toward the booth, she'd clobber him. "Come back any time, now."

He smiled. Not likely.

He pushed open the door and a bell jingled. He didn't remember hearing it when they walked in. That was odd.

"Jeremy," Greta called out. "Text me when you're home. So I know you made it safe. Okay?"

His mouth dry, he didn't attempt replying. He gave a nod as he let the door close. He climbed onto this moped and put on his helmet. Taking too long with the straps, his hands fumbling with aligning connectors, he left them as is and push started the bike. He rode away.

It was also sad knowing he wouldn't be back. That had truly been, not just the best pizza, but the best food he'd ever eaten.

Chapter 24

Tuesday, September 27th

A sudden noise jarred Jeremy awake. He sat up in bed and looked around. The bedroom was dark. The fuzzy sensation of sleep lingered. Closing his eyes, he tried shaking his head for clarity. He couldn't remember having gone to sleep in his room. He should be on the sofa. That was where he slept the last several days.

Uncle Jack.

He had started out on the sofa. Uncle Jack woke him, convincing him to go up to his room. He'd been too sleepy to argue and agreed.

At least he thought it might have happened that way.

Bottom line was simple. He wasn't on the sofa in the living room. He was upstairs in his room. The lights were off. And a loud noise woke him.

He couldn't recall the sound. A bang? A scrape? Had something shattered?

Had the sound originated in his room? On the other side of the closed door?

Slowly, his eyes adjusted. The darkness still consumed the room but less of it. Thankfully, a bright moon sent beams backlighting closed blinds.

He stared at the wall opposite his bed.

A dark shadow in the corner moved.

Jeremy wanted to close his eyes. He wanted to lie down and pull the sheets over his head. Hiding from whatever was in the room with him made the most sense.

He kept his eyes open. Unblinking, he stared into the darkness.

There was a shape. A person's shape.

His heart beat faster and faster. It thudded painfully against the inside of his chest. He wondered if a beating heart could crack ribs?

Getting out of bed and making a dash for the door was out of the question. His muscles, his legs, felt paralyzed. He didn't think he could stand if he jumped out of bed, much less dash across the room.

Something glowed in the corner of the room. Two small orb-like lights. Only they weren't lights, but more incandescent. The orbs, floating halfway up the wall, blinked out.

Jeremy hoped it was over and found strength for pushing himself backward in bed, pressing his shoulders against the wall. He never looked away from the corner of the room.

A howling came from outside as the wind picked up. Swaying tree branches cast shadows onto the closed blinds. The house creaked and moaned.

Jeremy's body was covered in sweat. His t-shirt stuck to his skin and was soaked through. He couldn't stop shivering. His teeth chattered. The room felt icy cold even though the thermostat read 68 degrees.

The orbs, marble sized and almond shaped, returned. Fainter this time.

They grew in size and then grew brighter in intensity.

Jeremy heard something whimper and drew the sheets toward his chest. He shook his head and wished he were dreaming.

The shadow stepped forward. "Where is she?"

The orbs were eyes. *Her* eyes and were now illuminated, bright white and locked on him. Her hands were raised like claws and she snarled as she charged forward.

With no luck, Jeremy tried pressing himself through the wall. His bare feet skidded down cotton sheets. As she reached the bed and launched into the air, he rolled to the right. Falling off the bed, he struck his head on the wall. The solid thud echoed inside his skull, bouncing around between his ears.

The only thing Jeremy could do was chance scrambling for the door. Pushing his fear aside was far easier said than done. Realizing his survival, his sanity, depended on action, he sucked in a deep breath and moved as fast as dragging himself across the floor would allow. As he rounded the foot of the bed, the woman's head appeared over the end with eyes now red as fire. Dark drool spilled from the corners of her mouth, like liquid mud mixed with coffee grounds. Her hands were on the footboard. Long fingernails carved into the wood as she pulled herself forward.

As Jeremy struggled getting up onto his feet, she sprung forward. When she crashed onto his back, he flattened on the floor. Aside from a crushing weight, it felt as if a block of ice laid across his entire body. His skin burned from the frigid cold encasing him. With his cheek pressed against the hardwoods, he saw his breath plume in front of his nose. In contrast, an intense heat rose from the nape of his neck. The drool was hot and rolled over his skin and down his back.

Palms down, Jeremy pushed up and rolled to one side, in an attempt at bucking the woman-thing off of him. He slid his legs forward and managed getting onto his knees. Throwing his arms up and back, he fought at freeing himself from her clutches. His body was in a torrent of pain that pulsed inside his veins and arteries, as much as it did over every inch of his skin.

Finally free and stumbling, Jeremy fell forward toward the door. His hand clasped around the knob and twisted as the woman-thing got to her feet. He couldn't look away as she slowly lifted her head and once again, locked eyes on him.

He pulled open the door. Only darkness on the other side filling in from the hallway. His legs wouldn't respond.

She lunged toward him.

That was the encouragement he needed. Jeremy flung himself out of the room and slammed the door closed in the woman-thing's face.

The hallway light came on.

The sudden brightness made him wince and he threw an arm up shielding his eyes.

"Jeremy! What the hell are you doing?" Jack was in the doorway of his bedroom. Jack's hand was still on the hall light switch. "Jeremy!"

* * *

There was no going back to sleep. Jack fried eggs on the stove, while Jeremy buttered toast. They worked in silence. Jeremy removed orange juice from the refrigerator and filled two glasses. Jack took two forks out of a drawer and placed them on the table. Jeremy stood by Jack with a plate in each hand.

"Over easy," Jack said, sliding three eggs into each plate. He wore a huge smile. "Dab the corner of your toast into the centers and the golden yolks will spill."

"They look perfect." Jeremy sat down, dipped his toast and just as his uncle promised, the yolk pooled onto the egg whites. Mopping the yolk with his toast, he took a bite. "Taste even better."

They each salted and peppered their eggs.

Jack held a fork in one hand. A messy piece of toast in the other. "Here's the thing. I'm worried about you. When you're not sleeping on the couch, you're having these nightmares in your room. I mean, I have nightmares now and then. What you have though, the screaming and running around the house, I'm not sure what to do about them."

Jeremy knew how sleeping problems were handled at St. Mary's. The patients went on a heavy prescription regime. It might be best for them to stay asleep at night, but it also left them like zombies all day long. His own prescriptions were strong enough. Thing was, he never felt sluggish, or not in control. "Can I ask you something?"

Jack used the side of his fork and cut the whites off around the yolk of an egg, folded it over and stuffed it into his mouth. "You know you can."

Jeremy's options were limited. St. Mary's might be the best place for him. If he was losing his mind, maybe his uncle would see it. Although he loved being away from the hospital, Fort Keeps just didn't feel like home anymore. "Thing is, once I ask you I can't take it back."

"Take it back?"

Setting down his fork, Jeremy said. "I think this house is haunted."

Jack chewed slowly. He sat back in his chair. When he lifted the glass of orange juice to his lips, his eyes scanned the ceiling. He drank down the juice and wiped his forearm across his mouth. "I'm pretty sure it is."

It wasn't what Jeremy expected. His eyebrows arched. "You're pretty sure … what?" He had to ask. It was all too possible that Uncle Jack had misheard him. He wasn't sure he had the courage to repeat those six words.

Jack's hands gripped the edge of the table and then palms smoothed over the top of the tablecloth. "This place. I agree with you. I'm pretty sure it's haunted. I debated selling the house, I did."

"Because it was haunted?"

Jack nodded. "It really isn't mine to sell. The house is yours. Besides, I had pretty much convinced myself it was just me. That I was seeing things." He leaned in close. "I wasn't going to tell anyone I was hearing noises or seeing ghosts."

"You see her?"

"A woman? A ghost? No. I haven't seen anything like that."

"Then what?"

"Things are moved. Cabinet doors found open, kitchen chairs found in the living room. Lights on, when I know they were off. Or lights off, when I know I had them on. And the noises, at night, the noises. At first, I'd have sworn it was just the sounds an old place like this makes." Jack shook his head, combed fingers through already messy hair. "Then, last couple of years, it settled down. In fact, it's been awhile since anything out of the ordinary has happened, until…"

Jeremy pursed his lips. "Until I came back?"

"It kind of seems that way. Like I was saying, I wanted to sell the place, but what if it was all in my mind? That wouldn't be fair to you. This was your parents' home. You grew up here." Jack picked up his fork again and pushed eggs around on the plate. "I figured, with you coming home, I'd figure out if I was going crazy or not."

Mental illness could be hereditary. "You're definitely not going crazy, Uncle Jack. Unless…"

"Unless, what?" Jack scooped an egg and placed it onto his toast and folded it in half. Yolk dripped out from between crusts.

"Unless *we* are."

Chapter 25

Jeremy showered with the bathroom door propped open and dressed with his bedroom door propped open. The best thing about the conversation he had with his uncle was the conclusion they'd reached. They'd make some minor repairs, paint some rooms, contact a realtor and have the house listed for sale.

This wasn't Jeremy's home any more than his room at St. Mary's.

After zipping up his jeans, he snatched his phone off of the dresser where it had been charging. Greta had called several times. She didn't leave a message, though. Ten texts from her waited behind a flashing blue light in his in-box. He stuffed the phone into his pocket.

Perhaps the thought of moving away from Greta would have convinced him keeping the house was better, but after his behavior the other night he'd done a one-eighty and now believed getting as far from Fort Keeps as possible would be best for everyone.

Eyeing the back corner of his bedroom suspiciously, *expectantly*, Jeremy edged his way out of the room, down the hall and down the stairs looking over his shoulder the entire time. Uncle Jack had already left for work just before he'd jumped in the shower. Part of him wanted his uncle to hang around until he finished washing. It didn't matter if his uncle would have understood. There was no way he was going to admit such cowardice. It could be weeks before they even put the house up for sale. He needed a way for coping with fear when alone in the house, that or pitch a tent in the yard.

If it were summer still, that might have been a viable option.

There was a flash of light that lit the living room. It came from out front. The brightness of the light gave Jeremy pause. He stared at the picture window and then jumped back two steps when the boom of thunder followed.

The sky must have been torn open by the slice of lightning. All at once, rain came down. It pounded the roof and awning.

It wasn't time for work. There were still a few hours to kill. Thing was, Jeremy wanted out of the house. The rain was a deterrent and could even prove dangerous on his moped.

Another bolt of lightning lit the sky as ˈit cut across bleak, dark storm clouds. This time thunder resonated in a long, growing growl. Once the crescendo was reached, the cacophony faded into crackles and grumbles.

Never hide under a tree when there is lightning around. In the Adirondacks there is nothing but trees. Walking to town was out of the question.

His leg vibrated. Startled, he lifted a foot off the ground, knee bent, as if he were about to slap a tarantula off his thigh.

It was his phone. He checked the display. Greta. Another text.

He sat on the sofa and read through her messages. She was worried about him. That was what it all came down to.

Sorry about how I acted. Hit send.

She wrote, *U avoiding my calls?*

Left my cell on the charger all night.

R U OK?

Yes.

I want to know what happened yesterday!! She wrote and then immediately sent: *Workin 2day?*

Yeah. He ignored her first comment and hoped he'd get away with the slight.

:-(

Jeremy smiled. *Why? U off?*

I am!!! Call in.

Although tempting, it wasn't the best idea. He'd already played the sick card. Barry deserved his best. *Can't. C U when I get out?*

That works. Come 2 the cafe.

Jeremy looked outside. The rain appeared furious. The wind, equally perturbed. Whether he took the moped or walked into town, he was going to get drenched. He thought about a change of clothes. Getting them from his room required him to go back upstairs. He believed all his bravery had been spent showering and getting dressed.

I'll either be wet or stink like pots & pans.

Doesn't bother me. If you care, bring a change of clothes.

He looked toward the staircase, sighed. Sounds good. *C U then.*

We're gonna talk about yesterday!

He stared at her message. Started to type out a few replies, most telling her to forget about getting together. Then he backed out the words. Finally he tapped out: *Fine* and hit send.

Standing, he pocketed his phone and braced himself for climbing the staircase.

Lightning flashed. At the top of the stairs he saw shadows dance across the hallway. The thunder clap shook the windows.

"Forget this." Jeremy snatched his keys and jacket and while embracing his cowardice, dashed out of the house and into the storm.

* * *

Jeremy thought for sure the rain would have stopped by the end of his shift. His coat hadn't completely dried from the ride into work. He winced as he pushed his arms through cold, wet sleeves. When he and Barry stepped out of the back of the diner, it was still coming down. The fifty degree temperature didn't help. He zipped up his coat and hugged himself.

"You be safe riding that thing home," Barry said, wagging a finger at the moped. "Wanna toss it in the back of my truck? I'll give you a lift. Roads could be slick. You break your neck, I have to hang a Help Wanted sign in the window. Got you already broke in. Hate to have to start over. What do you think?"

Greta wanted to meet up. Despite how tired he felt after working hard all day, he didn't plan on missing the date. Jeremy said, "I appreciate the offer. Don't think I'm headed home just yet, though."

Barry gave him a wide grin, a thumbs up. "I get ya. You just promise me you'll be safe. And for Heaven's sake, don't take her for a ride on that bike. Not tonight. Not in this. Roads up here are tricky enough. After all of this rain, could be washed out. Mud slides."

"You have my word. We're just meeting up for coffee."

"Coffee." Barry's grin grew. Then his jaw set. He pointed a finger. "Be safe and be careful. Hear me?"

"Loud and clear."

"Good job tonight. Busy night. Rain brings them out. Not sure why. People like going out to eat when it rains, I guess. You kept up very well." Barry climbed into his truck. "Put your helmet on!"

Barry gave his horn a honk as he pulled out of the back lot.

Jeremy regretted not having a change of clothing. He'd still be wet, but he wouldn't feel as dirty. There was an odor that came from scrubbing pots, pans and dishes. It was difficult to describe. If he smelled his hands it reminded him of spoiled meat marinated in soap. An overall pungent stench.

Too late now, regardless. He didn't have a change of clothing. He was soaking wet already and it was time to head down to the cafe.

Jeremy parked his moped in front of Paparazzi's. He didn't know how busy the cafe had been all day, but right now they were dead. Unlike the diner, it seemed people didn't leave their house for coffee.

He ran for the cafe door. It made no sense, rushing. He was already soaked. Walking, or running into the cafe had absolutely no bearing on the matter. Still, rushing for the door was what he'd done.

As he walked in, flashbulbs popped.

He was a star!

The walls inside Paparazzi's were decorated with black and white glossies of countless actors, actresses and famous musicians. A glass showcase displayed more valued memorabilia. The boxing gloves Jon Voight wore in the movie, *The Champ*, dangled over the bowling shoes

Andrew McCarthy wore in *Mannequin.* A framed silver record and plaque of the Go-Go's triple platinum *Beauty and the Beast* hung mounted inside the case behind Snake Plissken's well-worn brown leather coat.

There was so much more, but Jeremy felt uncomfortable roaming around the cafe reading about each of the different items.

"Can I help you?" A woman stood behind the counter. The hair. The eyes. The smile. He recognized her at once. The nameplate she wore read, *Erica.*

"I'm here to see Greta?"

The woman frowned. "Are you Jeremy Raines?"

Had Greta talked about him to her mother? He tried not to smile. There was a slight chance Greta liked him—liked him in the same way he liked her—but he wasn't sure. She could just be a nice person. She might just consider him a friend.

Even if she did like him, she'd had boyfriends before. He'd never really talked with a girl, except when trying to get CarryAnn not to eat the *Sorry* game pieces at St. Mary's. He held out his hand and on the inside, cringed, hoping she couldn't smell him. "Yes, ma'am. It's nice to meet you."

"Well, I'm confused." Her brow furrowed. "I got a text from her this morning. Said she was spending the day with … you?"

With me? Jeremy frowned. If she had made plans, behind her parents' back and used him as an alibi, as an excuse, he didn't want to say the wrong thing. The last thing he wanted was for her to get in trouble. However, she could have told him. He was now in something a tough spot.

Was she with Kevin?

He was like the only other person he knew in town, which was sad.

"Was she with you today?" Her expression deflated. Concern was apparent, as she looked at him, studied him, expectantly.

Jeremy almost felt trapped. He didn't want to lie to this woman. It was important always to tell the truth. Covering for his only friend also felt vital. He felt pulled in opposite directions. There was no easy answer. If he could move back time, he could avoid walking inside the cafe.

That was fantasy, though. Time Travel. "Ms. Murray…"

She pulled a phone from her apron. "I'm calling the police." She dialed, then looked toward the back of the cafe. "Abe? Abe!"

A door swung open.

Erica said, "Yes? I need to see an officer." She gave the Paparazzi Cafe name and address, as well as her phone number.

"What's going on?" Abe wore a white apron. It looked brand new. Wrinkle-free. He dried his hands on a white hand towel. His stared at Jeremy.

Jeremy initially thought the question was meant for his wife. He stood in front of the counter feeling awkward and uncomfortable.

Erica placed a trembling hand on her husband's forearm. "The reason I want to see an officer? I think something may have happened to my daughter."

Chapter 26

Jeremy's legs nearly gave out. He leaned forward, reached for the counter for balance. Erica Murray was on the phone with 9-1-1. Allegedly, Greta had told her mother that the two of them were spending the day together.

"She's eighteen." Erica squeezed her husband, Abe's, arm as if tapping into his energy for strength and maybe courage. "No, she's not on any medication. No. No diagnosed mental health issues."

Erica made accusatory eye contact with him while answering the questions asked.

Greta's mother made Jeremy feel apprehensive, though. He felt jittery and he breathed quick, shallow breaths.

"No. She has not done this kind of thing before." Thankfully, Erica went back to feeding information to the 9-1-1 telecommunicator. Her face reddened and through clenched teeth she said, "Can I please just get an officer out to my cafe now? These questions aren't helping find my daughter!"

"You got something to do with this?" Abe asked, dropping the hand towel onto the counter and then put his hands on his hips, all the while never looking away from Jeremy. The man was imposing, no doubt.

Inadvertently, Jeremy took a step back and pointed at himself. "Me? No, sir."

Erica Murray hadn't given Jeremy enough time to decide what he should do. He could have said that Greta spent the day with him. Lying didn't sit right in his mind. Except for a white lie told now and then at St. Mary's, he'd been brought to believe lying was wrong and always caused more problems. Trouble, even.

His indecision prompted Erica to call the sheriff.

That was probably best. Just because he didn't care for O'Sullivan, the man was a trained professional. That was exactly what the Murray's needed right now, someone who could actually react, do something and eventually shed light on the situation.

"I don't know what she was wearing last," Erica said. "She was in bed still when I left for work. So, pajamas, I guess. That's the last thing I saw her in. Eighteen, I told you that already. M-A-R-G-A-R-E-T-A Murray."

Abe finally looked at his wife. "I didn't see her either, honey."

Erica disconnected the call and set her phone down on the hand towel. "Did she message you, or call you at all today?"

Jeremy dug out his phone. His arm shook. He held the phone with both hands. "Yeah. Ah, yes, I mean. Yes, she did."

Abe asked, "When was that? When was the last time?"

"It was this morning. We texted," Jeremy touched his phone screen and opened up the text conversation between them. There was nothing to hide. He showed his phone to Greta's parents.

They huddled close and read the exchange.

Abe arched an eyebrow and went back to staring at Jeremy. "You're the Raines kid?"

Jeremy picked up his phone. "Maybe I should be going?"

Abe moved fast. He came around the counter and blocked the front exit. "I think it might be better if you wait for the sheriff."

Jeremy didn't want another encounter with the Fort Keeps law. "This has nothing to do with me."

Erica managed to look both angry and sad. She had tears rolling down her cheeks, but the snarl made her upper lip and half of her nose twitch. "She told me she was spending the day with you. She's an adult, really. She could do anything she wanted; so why lie? Why make something up? There wasn't a reason for her to so. Why tell me she's with you all day, if she wasn't going to be with you all day?"

Jeremy's stomach flopped about inside his gut. The tone of this conversation shifted. He felt like prey in a dangerous lair. "I can't answer that," he said, not at all sure he understood the questions.

Should he mention Kevin?

Maybe the parents didn't care for Kevin. If that were the case, it would be easier for Greta if she said she planned on spending the day with anyone else other than Kevin. Him even, if it pacified judgmental looks, or invasive questions later.

The room felt like it was getting smaller. The walls moved, boxing him in.

In no time at all, he'd feel weight of the entire building. The encroaching walls made his breathing labored. Removing clothing helped in situations like this. Sweat brimmed across his forehead.

He lost his balance and wobbled toward the right.

Abe struck faster than Jeremy thought possible. The man's arm shot forward and his hand locked on Jeremy's wrist. "You're not going anywhere. Wait until the police get here. After they talk to you about where my daughter is and then they let you leave, fine. Until then," Abe said, turning Jeremy around. "Why don't you take a seat?"

* * *

Jeremy sat by the front window in the cafe after the Sheriff O'Sullivan and Deputy Sierra Mendoza entered the cafe. Mendoza was tall, thin. She had copper colored skin and a crisp, pressed uniform. The officers stood by the counter and spoke with the Murrays. Words made it across the cafe, softly, but the voices carried. Most of what they said he was able to hear.

"You tried calling Greta's phone?" O'Sullivan asked. The deputy flipped open a memo pad and with pen poised, waited to take down what was said.

"I called it repeatedly and I've sent I don't know how many unanswered texts." Erica tossed hands into the air displaying disbelief and frustration.

Abe Murray leaned close towards the officers. He whispered. Jeremy couldn't pick up a single sound. He turned away from the four of them as all four of them turned and looked over at him. He stared out the window. The rain had finally stopped. A small, steady stream ran down the side of the street.

O'Sullivan dropped a foot onto the chair across from him; he leaned forward and rested an arm across his thigh.

Hairs on Jeremy's arm stood on end. Smoothing them over with a hand didn't keep them down.

"You look pretty nervous about something," the sheriff said. "Care to tell me what's on your mind?"

He'd seen enough television shows at the hospital. Talking to the police without an attorney present was never a good idea. Cops were trained in interrogation techniques. They knew how to coax answers out of people. Suspects. Jeremy felt targeted. "I'm just wondering—"

"Huh?" O'Sullivan pressed a finger behind his ear, bent in closer. "Speak up."

Jeremy cleared his throat. All eyes were on him. "I said, I was just wondering why no one is out looking for Greta."

"Got a place for us to start looking?"

Jeremy shook his head.

"No? No idea where we should go to find Greta?"

Jeremy looked up, met O'Sullivan's scrutiny head on. "No, sir."

"How about your phone?"

"What about it?" Jeremy put a hand over his leg, felt the phone under his palm in his pocket.

"I understand you were *texting* with Greta this morning?" The way he said texting made the act seem unnatural and sound offensive. The sheriff's left eye twitched.

Jeremy almost felt guilty admitting he had been texting with Greta. He'd done nothing wrong. Everyone texted. "I was."

"You make plans to meet up?" Again, the insinuation was that making plans was wrong and frowned upon. The accusation was implied, but felt directly aimed at him.

"We did."

The sheriff grinned. It was as if he had made points with his questions and was getting closer to some deep, dark truth. "So when was the last time you saw her?"

Jeremy didn't need a moment to think before answering, but he took one. His mouth felt dry. His tongue felt swollen and pressed against the roof of his mouth as he swallowed. Dr. Burkhart sometimes made him feel this way. Grilling him with a line of questions that clearly led somewhere, but only the doctor knew the direction and more importantly, the destination. "Last night."

O'Sullivan nodded his head. The way he did it, head tilted to the side, told Jeremy the sheriff wasn't buying the answer. "Last night? Is that right? Not today?"

Jeremy shook his head.

"I can't hear a head shake."

"No. Not today." This was getting too intense. Jeremy wanted his uncle. He didn't feel comfortable having the sheriff interrogate him. He'd seen enough television in the hospital to know his rights. It wasn't that he confused reality and fantasy. He knew TV shows were just TV shows. Still, he learned from the programs he watched. "I think I want to talk to my uncle."

"Your uncle? Yeah. Sure. We can give him a call. I planned on getting him down here, anyway." O'Sullivan stood up tall and ran his thumbs around the inside of the waistband on his uniform slacks. "Just tell me this. What time did you go into work today?"

He'd asked for his uncle, not an attorney. Maybe the sheriff could keep asking questions as long as he didn't lawyer up. He wasn't positive, though. He didn't have an attorney. Maybe Uncle Jack did? "I went into work, I think just before noon."

"You think?"

"I don't know exactly. I punch in. Barry would know. He could look at my timecard."

"We'll do that."

Why would they do that? Why did they care about what time he started work? "Can I call my uncle?"

"Just a minute, son. First, I want to hear what you did before work. You had the entire morning to yourself. How'd you spend that time?" Sheriff O'Sullivan rested a palm on the butt of his holstered handgun.

"It was raining."

"Yes. It was."

Jeremy thought about how long he'd stayed in the house, much longer than he had wanted to, before running out into the rain, away from whatever was watching him inside. How long had he stood under the tall tree in front? He wished the swing his father put up had still been there. He was too big for it. The rope would have snapped after all these years, for sure. Instead and against his better judgment, he kept his back to the bark and just stared at the house. "I slept in. Got ready. Went to work. It's pretty much the same thing I do every day. Why?"

O'Sullivan swooped in close. They were nose to nose. Jeremy had to blink to clear the suddenly blurred vision. The sheriff ground his teeth. He whispered, "Are you asking the questions now? Huh, are you?"

"I just want to call my uncle. I'm seventeen, you know." He thought his age might make the difference. He thought seventeen was a minor. It worked that way in police shows he'd seen. Parents, or an attorney, would show up and pull the suspect out of the interrogation room, scolding the detectives for questioning a minor without a parent, or counsel present.

"You don't belong here. How they let someone like you out of the loony bin is beyond me. Beyond me!" The sheriff looked like he was about to say something more, ask something else. His nose and eye twitched this time. And then he backed away. Slow. And stood up. "Why don't you call your uncle? Have him come down here."

"And then I can go?"

"And then you can answer some more questions!"

* * *

Jeremy sat alone by the window in the cafe. His own reflection, obscured by drops of rain rolling down the glass filled his field of vision. The sheriff loomed over his deputy, talked fast, but too low for Jeremy to overhear a word.

The front door opened. Jack Raines walked in. He stopped as flashbulbs *pop pop popped.* He scanned the cafe. "Jeremy," he said and strode toward his nephew. "Come on. We're out of here."

The sheriff beat him over to stand next to Jeremy and placed a hand on Jeremy's shoulder. "Not so fast."

"Are you charging him with anything?"

O'Sullivan was silent.

Jack said, "How long have you been here, Jer?"

Jeremy shook his head. He didn't know. Felt like hours. Could have been days. He wasn't sure.

"You've been questioning a minor?"

"We were talking." O'Sullivan was quick with his answer this time.

"Is he charged with anything?"

"We don't know that a crime has been committed. Yet." O'Sullivan, again, rested his hand on the butt of his weapon. Chest puffed. "You want to take him home? Take him home. I'm sure I'm going to have more questions."

Jack signaled for Jeremy. "We're out of here."

Jeremy got to his feet. He inched his way past the sheriff. Inside he waited for O'Sullivan, expecting a hand would clamp down over his shoulder, detaining him. It didn't happen. A sigh escaped him once he was beside his uncle. It hissed out of his mouth like a slow bicycle tire leak.

Chapter 27

The bunk inside the cell was mounted into the wall, without legs, it hovered a few feet above the ground. He laid on his back, but there was no getting comfortable on an inch thin mattress. Caleb hadn't been sleeping anyway. The dark never bothered him as much as it did since he and his brother had been confined inside the jail. Some candle light was visible through the small glass window on the door leading into the sheriff's office. A window or two wouldn't have hurt. If the law was worried about people escaping, bar them. No reason why sun- and moonlight should be prohibited. They hadn't been convicted of any crime at this point. Innocent until proven guilty must not apply in the mountains.

Caleb placed his forearm across his eyes. He knew Jacob couldn't see him, but just in case, he wanted his tears hidden. Going home and working the land with his father was all he thought about. When he did sleep, it was what he dreamt of, too. He could not imagine being locked inside a cage for the rest of his life, not even for the rest of the month. Not even for the rest of the night.

When Caleb turned onto his side, his eyes caught movement by the door. Something had been standing in front of the small square of glass, blocking the little light allowed.

He couldn't determine on which side of the door the movement occurred. Part of him wanted to call out, asking who was there. He kept his mouth closed, though. Jacob had no issue sleeping. If he woke Jacob over nothing, his brother would never let it go. It wasn't really a good thing, but at least locked away in separate cells he wasn't as afraid of getting knocked around for doing what Caleb called *stupid things*.

That was definitely the only good thing about their situation, though. The only good thing. If there were any other benefits to being locked behind bars, he couldn't think of a one. Not for lack of trying. Day in and day out he wracked his brain for some silver lining he could hold onto.

What made it worse was when their father stopped down to see them the other day.

Caleb clung so tightly to the bars his knuckles turned white; he pressed his head between the cold iron until his ears ached. If his head were just a tad smaller he could probably push it through the narrow gap. "Where's Ma? She come down with you, Pa? Is she out there waiting to see us, too?"

"Calm yourself," Jacob snapped. He stood in his cell, slouched and bent forward. His arms, askew, dangled between the bars in a lackadaisical fashion. "Act like a man, would you?"

Their father held his hat in both hands, slowly turning the brim around and around. "I couldn't do it to her, Caleb. I didn't want her any more heartbroken than she is now. Seeing the two of you locked in here like dogs, it would kill her dead."

"Quit your crying." Jacob didn't hold back. He clutched the bars and twisted his body as if he thought he could remove the iron from the floor and ceiling with brute strength. "He's like a baby, Pa. Always crying. Half the night I have to listen to him over there sniffling and sobbing. I don't know how much more of it I can take."

Their father motioned with a hand. "Well let's settle down, the three of us. This ain't easy for no one. I'm just here to see how you all are doin'?"

"You going to be able to get us out of here?" Caleb asked. He used his soiled shirt sleeve as a handkerchief and ran his arm under his nose. "We going to be able to come home soon?"

"I'm doing what I can. I've been down to Herkimer County and met with the solicitor there. These kinds of things cost money. Being that there is two of you looking to defend…"

"You're going to pay the man, aren't you, Pa?"

Caleb was thankful his brother asked the question. It was the same one he'd have asked, but thought Jacob would have yelled at him again. And although it was the question he would have asked, he knew it was unnecessary. His parents weren't going to let their boys rot away in the Clinton Correctional Facility. Rumors about that place spread worse than tuberculosis.

A scraping noise pushed him out of the memory.

Had he been falling asleep?

He sat up, but was still in bed. He didn't dare dangle legs off the side of the cot. The darkness felt too alive for that. Where was Jacob?

Had he heard the scraping sound? Had he seen the shadow pass in front of the door?

Someone *was* moving around in the darkness. Something was watching him.

"Jacob? Jacob is that you?" Caleb hoped it was. He spent days watching his brother pace around inside his cell. Usually Jacob mumbled while he walked, counting off points, or punching a fist into a palm. Wasn't it likely that Jacob couldn't sleep and was pacing through the night?

Very likely.

Then why didn't he answer me? Caleb wondered.

He was about to call out to his brother a second time, but when he heard keys rattle he clamped his mouth shut. His body trembled. Whatever moved in the darkness had stopped in front of his cell door.

He saw the subtle outline of a shadow. The dark was blacker where *whoever* was out there stood.

A key was thrust into the keyhole.

Caleb's teeth chattered. A chill raced through his body.

Hinges whined as the cell door swung outward.

It was in the cell with him.

He heard it breathing. Hard. Heavy.

Or was it his own labored breathing he heard?

Enough was enough. He opened his mouth to scream.

Searing pain sliced through the corners of his mouth. He clapped a hand over the lacerating wounds. Warm blood spilled from his face and out from between his fingers. Blood ran down his arms. In defense, he threw up his free hand. He could not see the attacker. He felt nothing waving his arm around. The darkness swelled around him.

Blood pooled in the back of his throat. More poured out of the sides of his mouth. His neck was wet with thick, hot blood. It flowed over his chest.

He couldn't scream. He couldn't call for help. He was unable to make a sound.

Something was plunged into his gut.

The sudden shock of the stabbing pain dropped him down onto his back.

The darkness rose over him.

He saw the hint of a face under a hood.

A ghost?

A monster?

A demon released from the gates of hell. It came for him specifically. He didn't have to ask what it wanted.

His arms reflexively shot upward as the demon punched holes in his chest. He twisted his head left and right as his skin split open. A burning numbness passed over his torso.

His energy flowed out of his body.

Caleb tried warning his brother, but gagged as only blood sputtered and sprayed from his mouth instead of sound, or words. He choked, unable to cough his lungs clear.

His skin felt as if it was on fire. Although there were no flames dancing on his flesh, he knew his body burned.

* * *

Jacob screamed. "Sheriff! Sheriff O'Sullivan! Someone! Anyone!"

He repeated the cry over and over.

The door at the front of the jail opened. Benji O'Sullivan ran into the jail, gun drawn.

"Nearly gave me a heart attack," the sheriff said, pushing his revolver into the holster on his gun belt. "It's dawn, Jacob. Just dawn. What are you already hollering about?"

Jacob, for the first time he could recall, was unable to speak. Instead, he pointed.

He watched the sheriff look over at Caleb's cell.

The cell was covered in blood. The only way Jacob could think to describe his brother's corpse was to call it shredded. Something had shredded his older brother.

The sheriff whispered. "Lord, have mercy."

Chapter 28

Jeremy gave Uncle Jack a rundown of everything that happened. His uncle didn't look happy about any of it and for a while, the two sat in silence at the kitchen table. The light bulb in the fixture overhead hummed.

"So that was the last you heard from her? The text?" Jack said.

"Yeah. Nothing since."

Jack said, "Have your phone?"

For a split second, Jeremy thought the sheriff had his phone. He clapped a hand onto his pocket. It was there. He fished it out. "Here they are."

Jack took the phone, scrolled through the few messages. "And you didn't do anything between the time I left for work and you got to the diner?"

"I was in the rain."

Jack looked up at the light bulb, as if a ghost was humming. "I understand."

Jeremy went to the fridge. He poured them a couple of sodas and sat back down. "What am I supposed to do now?"

Leaning back in his chair, Jack pursed his lips. "There's nothing you need to do. Nothing. If the sheriff had anything conclusive, you wouldn't be here right now. You'd be locked up."

Jeremy shuddered. A jail cell sounded horrible. He couldn't imagine being locked away. He'd often considered St. Mary's a prison. He suddenly realized his assessments had been wrong. "I don't want to go to jail."

"You won't. Not going to happen." Jack drank the soda and smacked his lips as he let out a satisfying *ahhhh*. "In the morning, we'll take a ride down to Old Forge. Friend of mine is an attorney. He does like wills and contracts, boring stuff."

Jeremy drummed fingers on the table.

"Look," Jack said. "Head up to bed. Get some rest. Things are going to look better in the morning. One way or another, we're going to work through this."

The words sounded great. Jeremy just wasn't sure how much stock he should put into them. "I think I will try and get some sleep."

"That's a good idea."

There's no way he'd sleep. His uncle didn't need to know this, though. He'd become a burden. It might be his house they lived in, but it became increasingly difficult not recognizing that he had overstayed his welcome.

Things would get done in the morning. No doubt about it. They could go and talk with a lawyer in town, but Jeremy also wanted to broach the subject of going back to the hospital. It was all he knew. The world had moved too far ahead without him. He didn't fit into it anymore. It came down to more than struggling. He felt as if he were drowning. St. Mary's was an invisible lifeline. He'd be foolish ignoring the safety, and the sanctuary, the institution afforded.

Jeremy stood up, pushed in his chair and made his way toward the stairs. The wood creaked under his weight as he climbed them. The darkness at the top of the stairs was ominous, but at the moment his thoughts revolved around Greta.

Where was she?

Was she okay?

What happened?

It was those three thoughts, posed in a variety of ways that whipped about inside his mind; a whirlwind with enough force to rival a Midwestern F-5 tornado.

It was those thoughts, that is, until the shadows stirred.

The darkness swirled.

The movement gave him pause. He stayed on the second to last step and stared. Squinting, he tried his best seeing into the abyss in front of him. The little light from the kitchen at the bottom of the stairs and around the way did not reach beyond the third stair.

He was alone.

Uncle Jack could be behind him, beside him. Not in front of him, though. It didn't matter. He was alone.

He stood alone.

There was no going back downstairs. It couldn't be real. Whatever was, or was not in front of him, couldn't be there.

Greta had witnessed the activity, though.

Or had she?

It was in his mind.

St. Mary's was the only place for him. It was where he belonged.

Jeremy climbed the last stairs and pushed through the hallway.

Something scratched on the hardwood floor, as if scurrying away, pressing into a corner.

Jeremy opened his bedroom door. Moonlight from outside the window lit his room. He switched on the light, regardless and closed the door. His guitar case was on the bed.

He hadn't played his guitar since coming home.

It wasn't him that moved the guitar.

He looked around the room, as he walked toward it, and then stood over his bed. He lifted the clasps and opened the hard-shell case. All six strings were broken. Coiled up around the head, at the end of the neck.

Jeremy slammed the lid closed. Locked it. He pushed the guitar case under the bed. He dropped back, flopped onto the mattress. His head on the pillow and stared up at the ceiling, his arms out in a T.

Something cold touched his hand.

He pulled his arms in. The right arm had been dangling over the edge of the bed.

He brought his legs up.

Sitting on his knees, Jeremy panted and looked around the room. Of course he saw nothing. Whatever touched him was hiding under the bed. The door looked like it was miles away.

He closed his eyes and shook his head. It wasn't real. There was no ghost.

"You can save her." The voice was little more than a whisper. It barely reached his ears.

He leaned forward and looked over the edge. His guitar case was there. It shouldn't have been. He just slid it under the bed. *Under* it.

No.

It was his mind, his imagination. He could prove it. There was nothing under the bed. No one under it.

Jeremy gripped the mattress and lowered his head over the side. Lifting the draped bed spread, his mouth went dry. His tongue felt thick and swollen.

Just as he looked under the bed, the bedroom lights went out.

He saw something under the bed, though.

It moved.

Something reached for him.

He sprang back up!

"You can save her."

This voice. It was barely audible, because it wasn't coming from inside the bedroom.

It came from outside his window.

The bedroom light came back on. The shadows were chased away. Jeremy didn't waste a second. He leapt off his bed and was beside the light switch, needlessly.

Dropping down to the floor, palms flat, lowering his face until his cheek was less than an inch away from the hardwoods and peered under his bed.

Like he thought.

Nothing.

No one was under the bed.

And his guitar case…

He rose. Slowly.

The guitar case was on the bed, the lid open.

"You can save her."

He was on his knees and staring at the window. The voice he heard was definitely coming from outside. He got to his feet and made his way over. At the sill, he parted the thin curtains and peered outside.

At first he saw only his own reflection, against the light. He cupped his hands around his face and pressed them against the glass.

She was there. By the trees. "Greta," he whispered. "Don't move!"

She wouldn't be able to hear him.

He made a break for the door, ran down the hallway, down the stairs and out the front door. If Uncle Jack was still in the kitchen, if he had still been at the table, Jeremy didn't notice.

First thing he felt was the cold. It was snowing. Nothing stuck on the ground, yet. Large flakes. They floated rather than fell. Jeremy ran through them around the side of the house. "Greta!"

Once he reached the backyard, his eyes scanned the tree line.

Everything looked brighter from out of his bedroom window. The lights in the room made the difference. Looking up, he saw clouds snaking over the moon. The glow casted was nearly gone. "Greta?"

He had seen her.

No one had been under his bed, but someone had been standing between the trees.

It could only be Greta.

He raced forward, feet slipping on slick grass. His hand touched the ground and kept him from toppling. At the trees where he'd seen her, he stopped, spun around. If more snow had fallen, he'd see tracks, her footprints.

There was nothing.

She was gone.

He knew he'd started crying. "I'm losing my mind." Ignoring the brimming tears, he pressed fists against his forehead. "I'm losing my mind!"

"You can save her."

It was behind him. Jeremy turned. She was down by the creek. On the opposite side. "Greta! Stay there. Don't move. I'm coming. Stay right there!"

He started down the slope, watched his footing. His arms were outstretched, hands bounced off trees for balance. He ducked under branches, tilted his head to the side to protect his eyes.

At the creek bed, she stood just on the opposite bank, her back to him and, without a word, she ran through the trees.

Jeremy splashed through the creek. Icy water filled his boots. Soaked socks clung to his feet. His toes felt instantly numb. "Greta!"

Chapter 29

Fort Keeps, NY — Adirondacks — October 1912

Although it was not yet ten in the morning, Sheriff Benji O'Sullivan struggled with the reality in front of him. How could someone have snuck into the jail during the night and murdered the elder Gregory boy? The attack wasn't just for killing. There was more behind the violence. Seventeen year old Caleb Gregory had been viciously shredded, at some point, during the night and so far O'Sullivan didn't have a single clue as to who could have done it.

"I'm going to want to get this boy back to my place as soon as possible." Dr. John Marr stood inside the jail cell, arms crossed, eyes closed and massaging the bridge of his nose.

"I'll have him delivered right away, doc. Can you tell me anything?" Benji O'Sullivan stood just outside the cell, leaning his weight on the barred door. He needed a drink. There had not been a single day in his career where he'd ever wanted a fifth of whiskey more.

"Caleb Gregory was murdered. The wounds, as they are right now, look consistent with a large knife. I'll have to get him out of his clothing, clean away some of the blood before I can get much more detailed." Marr shook his head. "And his brother?"

"Swears he never heard a thing. I wasn't here last night. Deputy Haddocks pulled the graveyard shift. Although he claims he was awake at the desk all night..." O'Sullivan tilted his head one way and then the other. "I don't fault them if they sleep. Nothing going on, catch some Zzzzs."

"Haddocks is a good enough man. Doesn't own but two uniform shirts." Marr waved a hand, as if understanding the small piece of trivia was nothing shy of peculiar. "Told me once when I mentioned to him I should re-marry someday, if just for the luxury of having someone do my laundry. Anyway, my point being if Haddocks were responsible there'd be virtually no way of hiding the blood on his clothing. Unless he stripped down to his skivvies before the attack. Where is the deputy now?"

"Took his gun, his badge and sent him home." O'Sullivan saw Marr frown. "He's the only suspect I have right now. *Him* claiming he was awake all night doesn't help his case any. How'd someone get in here then and do this? But I'll ride out to his place. Check his shirts. If those check out, I'll have him return to work. Lord knows right now is not the best time to be short-handed."

"And Jacob was in his cell? Where is he now?"

"Have one of my deputies with him. Locked him in an ice cellar for now. Deputy has been instructed to sit in a chair on those cellar doors until I come and get him." Sheriff released a discouraging sigh. "Both cells were locked. Keys were out front on the hook. I don't see any way Jacob could have been involved. Between you and me, I'd love to tag this murder on him, too. Thing is, when I got here this morning, the deputy was sitting out front smoking. Feet up. I came in and just sat down when I heard him screaming. I have to tell you, kid was white as a ghost and scared something serious. He sweat more this morning than he did when questioned about Alice's murder."

"I guess his exhibiting fear is a good thing. Closer to remorse, I suppose," Marr said, arching an eyebrow.

They liked Jacob for the Crosby killing. Neither thought Caleb was equally responsible. He might have been there, but they suspected him more of a witness than a participant. They'd both have been locked away for twenty-five to life, but maybe only Jacob deserved it.

Now, unfortunately, Jacob would do his time and be released in his forties, while Caleb would only get buried six feet deep into the earth.

The sheriff stood up straight, walked into the cell. "I'm going to have him moved. Send him down to Herkimer County. Just for safekeeping."

Murdering a young girl didn't sit well with folks in Fort Keeps. He'd heard more than a few rumblings and people calling for the Gregory boys to be hung until dead. This wasn't the Wild West. Hell, it wasn't even the wild east. He'd let everyone know there wouldn't be a hanging.

Someone must have taken offense and rather than let a qualified judge and jury of peers decide the fate of the Gregorys, took matters into their own hands. "Going to be bad enough I have to tell the parents I failed at keeping their oldest safe. Moving Jacob is the best plan I have right now."

Chapter 30

Jeremy was breathing hard, heavy. His breath plumed in front of his face. From his bedroom window he had seen Greta by the trees in the backyard. He'd immediately gone outside looking for her. Now, she'd led him deeper into the woods.

None of the night made sense.

Nothing.

He couldn't understand why Greta didn't stay put, why she wouldn't just let him catch up to her.

He was shivering. He hugged himself, rubbed his arms with arms crossed over his chest. Somehow, he'd lost track of Greta.

He stopped moving. Just for a minute. He leaned his back against a tree.

Above him, he thought he heard an owl. It hooted.

His teeth chattered as he looked left and right. He wasn't sure how long he'd been chasing after her. Worse, he wasn't sure if he knew where he was. Lost wasn't the right word. He could find his way back home if he needed, maybe.

Ahead, he heard a branch snap. Underfoot. As if someone stepped on sticks.

He couldn't see anyone. The thick darkness enveloped everything.

"You can save her."

The voice was both behind him and in front of him. Jeremy pushed off and away from the tree. He thought he'd gone blind. He stopped forward, arms out, hands passing through air. "Who's there?"

It wasn't Greta.

It was never Greta.

"Where is she? Where's Greta?" He heard movement behind him. He turned fast.

Black. Night. Shadows.

He didn't know where he was. He was lost, turned around.

"You must save her."

Her. "Greta. Where is she?"

The apparition was there. Not close. Not clear. The image shimmied. She was at least thirty yards away. Was she glowing? How could he see her through the darkness?

She was above him. Not floating. She was on the slope.

As soon as he started toward her, she turned and began walking. Climbing.

Was the ghost from his house taking him to find Greta?

* * *

Fort Keeps, NY — Adirondacks — October 1912

Sheriff Benji O'Sullivan had no one to blame but himself. He'd let his guard down and hadn't been prepared for the ambush.

O'Sullivan planned on moving Jacob Gregory down to Herkimer County at dusk. There was no way telling if whomever had chopped his older brother, Caleb, into mincemeat, was planning on killing him, as well. And although it was a ten-million to one chance lightning struck twice in the jail, he'd feel better safe than sorry. Sometimes the crazier the likelihood, the more likely the possibility. Which didn't make sense, but how many things in life did?

After a talk with Deputy Haddock and verifying that his two uniform shirts didn't have blood and probably hadn't been washed in a week, or two, Dr. Marr worked on Caleb's autopsy. The man was busier with corpses the last few weeks than he was seeing patients for checkups. He supposed, like himself, the change in pace, in the nature of day-to-day work added an element to the job. O'Sullivan never wished for death, but couldn't deny two murders added a splash of that something missing to his life. He hated to say investigating a bizarre death was rather invigorating.

The sheriff wasn't comfortable with locking Jacob back in his cell at the office. Seemed like cruel and unusual punishment, even though Caleb's cell, the walls and floor had been scrubbed clean. Any sign of blood or scraps of filleted flesh had been removed and disposed of. Thing was if he had somewhere else to store the teenager he would have. He couldn't keep the boy locked in an ice cellar for too long.

Once O'Sullivan was sure Jacob was secured in a cell with Webb law enforcement in Old Forge, then he could return to Dr. Marr's for a more in-depth explanation around cause of death. He knew perfectly well stabbings killed the boy, but how many times was the kid stabbed? O'Sullivan was curious if Dr. Marr had any insight into the kind of psychotic lunatic that might be loose in the mountains.

They had been swamped the rest of the day and most of the evening. Having a deputy assigned to watch the locked cellar impeded his work delegation considerably. Like it or not, cruel and unusual or not, they brought Jacob back to the jail roughly an hour ago. Kid looked defeated. Cuffs kept his arms pinned behind his back. His head down, he shuffled through the office and into the jail as if his legs had been shackled as well.

Lifting the keys off the ring outside the door to the jail, Sheriff O'Sullivan decided now as good a time as any to head out. "It's time," he said.

Jacob didn't look any better. He sat Indian-style on the cot, arms and hands buried deep between his crossed legs, with his back to the cell Caleb had been locked in. A pang of guilt struck O'Sullivan. Maybe the ice cellar had been the better choice over the jail cell? It was too late now.

He unlocked the cell. "Ready, son?"

Jacob's head snapped around. "I am not your son!"

The skin around the boy's eyes were red, irritated and puffy. Under his nose was rubbed raw.

O'Sullivan let the outburst go. He saw no need in banter. Jacob murdered a young girl. The boy didn't deserve his sympathy. Despite the horrid acts committed, he still felt bad about how Caleb's death affected Jacob. He supposed it came down to compassion and empathy. When all of this was over, he'd reflect.

Helping Jacob off the cot, he led the boy out of the jail, through the office and outside where his horse was hitched to an uncovered wagon. Fire danced from a lit torch secured to an arm on the front of the wagon. They each climbed up onto the back of the wagon. Jacob sat on piled straw. O'Sullivan removed one cuff and re-secured it on Jacob's wrist after sliding the chain through an iron bar running the lengths of the wagon. "Got a blanket right here, in case you get cold."

For late October, it was a mild night. Clouds covered most of the night sky, hid most of the moon and almost all of the stars.

The sheriff climbed over the back of the wagon, sat on the seat, set his feet on the footboard and lifted the reins off of the brake. He made a click-click noise on the side of his mouth and snapped the reins.

A peacefulness overcame the sheriff as he settled in and somewhat enjoyed the ride. The horse hooves stepped in time, the rhythmic ca-clack ca-clack with the rolling of the wheels felt calming. Despite the list of things that needed doing, O'Sullivan tried letting go. The moment wouldn't last. Not taking advantage of the quiet would have been considered sinful.

Overhead, tree branches cracked and something rustled. Shaken leaves rained down. A large object dropped out of the tree. It crashed into the back of the wagon. Jacob screamed. Spooked, the horse galloped. O'Sullivan tugged on the reins and pressed on the brake with his left foot.

With the wheels locked up, the wagon swerved. Jacob's screams were blood curdling. O'Sullivan struggled gaining control of his horse and chanced a look back over his shoulder.

Once his horse stopped, and shook its head it neighed in protest. O'Sullivan snatched the torch from the hold and jumped into the back of the wagon.

Jacob was alone. Blood splatter was everywhere. The boy's eyes were open, staring up at nothing.

He heard someone, something, running.

He held his arm out. The flames from the torch barely lit the night in front of his face. The fire did nothing for penetrating the surrounding darkness.

Whatever had jumped into the back of the wagon had run into the woods.

O'Sullivan gave chase.

He breathed hard, heavy as he dodged branches and leapt over fallen limbs. He ducked and shielded his eyes from getting poked or scratched. He stopped. Standing still, he listened.

Sound was funny in the dark.

The noises he heard came from all around him.

He thought the sounds came from the north, as if headed back toward Fort Keeps. He pursued.

After twenty minutes of finding nothing, of coming across no one, he resigned. He bent forward, coughing. The torch flame had dwindled.

Standing up straight, he pivoted around.

He didn't hear anything. The woods were silent.

Creatures living among the trees didn't make a sound. It was as if collectively, they waited, watching him, wondering what his next move might be.

He had no move.

He was chasing a shadow.

Chapter 31

Jeremy heard his parents fighting. From upstairs he couldn't understand the words, couldn't place the context. His father yelled. Something slammed against something. A fist against the wall? A palm on the tabletop?

He stood at the bottom of the staircase, peeked around and into the kitchen. Sweaty hands held on tight to the railing post, his cheek resting against white knuckles. Cold tears rolled from his eyes. Blinking only blurred his vision.

His mother sat in a chair at the kitchen table with hands folded in her lap.

"How could you do this? How could you do this to me? To us? To Jeremy?" His father had his back to the door. His arm was up, hand planted on the cupboard. He leaned his weight on his arm, head dropped, deflated. "I just—I just don't get it."

"It's not what you think—"

His father slammed his hand against the cupboard. "Not what I think? It's not what I think? Are you kidding me?" The laugh came next. Jeremy could not find anything funny.

His mother stood up. She walked around the table, keeping distance between herself and his father. At the sink, she turned on the faucet. She shook her fingers under the water. She grabbed a glass out of the cupboard, filled it.

With trembling hands, she took a sip.

His father moved fast, stepped forward, pushed a chair out of the way and slapped the glass out of her hand. It shattered on the linoleum at the same time the toppled chair banged on the floor.

Jeremy jumped back, gasped. His lips quivered and he thrust his fingertips into his mouth. His nose ran and he sniffled. There was no looking away though. Every instinct inside him told him to run up into his bedroom. He should close the door and hide under his bed, or in a closet.

He didn't move away. Instead, he leaned forward again and took up his position against the post.

"Oh, really?" His father shook his head, had his hands on his hips.

"Get away from me." His mother's tone of voice was filled with an audible fear.

"Put that down. Honey, put that down right now!"

Jeremy's eyes opened wide. He couldn't see what his mother had in her hands. Was it another glass? Did she want more water? Why wouldn't his father let her have something to drink?

He, again, thought hiding might be best. He'd crawled under his bed a few days ago when his parents had been fighting. He still could hear the shouting. Pressing his hands against his ears kind of helped. Everything became muffled. He'd stayed under the bed with his eyes squeezed tightly shut, too. It wasn't until his mother found him, that he opened them. She coaxed him out, softly speaking to him, convincing him that everything was going to be okay.

Everything was not okay, though.

Hiding hadn't helped at all.

Watching his parents fight was worse. More than running upstairs, he wanted to race into the kitchen. They would stop fighting if they saw him. Jeremy knew he could fix the situation. He'd done it before. Last week when they were arguing and he walked into the room, they went silent. His father left, took the truck. He'd then sat on the sofa with his mother. They found something to watch on television together. She made hot cocoa and popped popcorn in the microwave for them to share.

Jeremy remembered staying up as late as he could, waiting for his father to come home. At some point he must have fallen asleep. He woke up the next day tucked into his bed. When he went downstairs the first thing he did was check out the front window. His dad's truck was in the driveway. It was the first time he could ever remember having been so scared and thought for sure his parents were going to divorce. Most of the kids at school came from homes where the parents were divorced. He didn't want that to happen with his family.

There was something different about the fighting this time. His legs kept him from moving. Jeremy wasn't sure he could go into the kitchen even if he wanted to, even if they had called him into the room. His entire body trembled.

His father lunged at his mother.

Jeremy opened his mouth to scream, but no sound came.

His parents became entangled. They banged against the table and into the counter.

"Drop it! Just drop it!" His father fumbled and twisted. He had Jeremy's mother by the wrists.

It wasn't a glass in her hand.

"Let me go!" His mother struggled, bending and turning. "You're hurting me!"

They fell into each other.

Something clattered onto the floor.

Jeremy didn't realize he'd been walking toward the kitchen. He wanted his parents to stop fighting. He wanted to yell at his father to leave his mother alone. Before, he said a word, the struggle ended.

His parents stood still.

"Oh, God," his father said.

His mother reached out over the sink. Her hand clutched at the thin, white curtains.

She stained them red. With wide, unblinking eyes, she stared at Jeremy's father. Her mouth was open.

No sound came from her, either.

Jeremy froze in place when his mother lost her balance. Her knees buckled. His father caught her, guided her body onto the floor. He ran his hand over her forehead, moving her hair away from her face.

"Oh, no," he said. "God, no."

And then the back door banged open...

"I didn't mean it." His father was crying, on his knees, splayed over his mother's unmoving body. "I swear. It was an accident. I didn't mean it."

* * *

Jeremy followed the apparition. He never gained any ground. She was always at least fifteen yards ahead of him. The darkness hid her now and then. As soon as he was about to stop, give up his pursuit, she'd reappear. She'd call to him, lead him deeper into the woods.

"Where are you taking me?"

The ghost kept telling him that he could save her.

Her.

It could only be Greta.

How would the ghost know anything about his friend?

Jeremy didn't have an answer. He feared everything happening was his fault. Greta never would have been exposed to the ghost if he hadn't have invited her into his house.

No. No. That made no sense at all.

There were no ghosts—no such thing as ghosts!

Then why am I following one, he asked himself. *Why am I risking freezing to death following some woman through the woods?*

Because, if there was even a chance that it truly was a ghost in front of him and that ghost knew something about Greta's whereabouts, he had to at least try.

It wouldn't be long before he was back in St. Mary's, anyway.

When this was over, whether he found Greta, or whether the sun rose, it would end. He was giving up. Surrendering.

He didn't belong in Fort Keeps.

The sheriff had been right.

"You can still save her…"

Chapter 32

Fort Keeps, NY — Adirondacks — October 1912

Sheriff Benji O'Sullivan thought he might be in shock. He had no idea what just happened. Someone—*something*—dropped out of the trees. Whatever it was, it had landed in the back of his wagon. The prisoner he was transporting, Jacob Gregory, was attacked.

No. It was more than that.

Jacob Gregory was dead. He'd been murdered.

As the law, he'd been unable to stop it.

Now, both of the Gregory brothers were dead. Both killed while in his custody.

The unusual murders pointed in one direction, at one particular person. Although Sheriff O'Sullivan didn't think it likely, not likely at all, he knew he needed to—at the very least—confront Elissa Crosby.

The Gregory boys were suspected in the murder of Elissa's young daughter.

Seemed probable she'd seek to extract her own revenge.

Having chased the person who just finished killing Jacob and losing them in the woods, the sheriff made his way back to the wagon. It was as if he'd been thrust into a nightmare. The people of Fort Keeps would call his competence as a sheriff into question once word spread two of his prisoners had been murdered while in his custody.

He tugged and yanked drawing a canvas over the corpse. Dr. Marr was going to be putting in for a lot overtime. Wouldn't be surprised if he called in for an assistant. Three bodies in such a short period of time made O'Sullivan think some kind of curse, like a storm cloud, was over the heads of all of Fort Keeps.

Facts were facts, though. They'd be right to demand his removal from office. He'd been unable to protect these two young men. He had no idea how he would face Mr. and Mrs. Gregory. Delivering news that now both of their boys were now dead…

He didn't want to think about it.

Couldn't allow himself to think about it. Not until after the killer was caught.

And he'd catch them!

Might be the last thing he ever did. Might not even be as sheriff, should he lose his position, but he'd not stop. He'd stop when he was dead or until they were captured.

He ignored the bloody mess and the mangled remains in the back of the wagon.

He climbed up onto the front seat and lifted the reins. He eased the horse around and headed back toward town.

* * *

The sheriff brought the horse to a stop in front of the Crosby place. The cold temperature was perfect for the corpse. Only thing O'Sullivan smelled was the gas coming from the horse's arse. A few times it nearly made him gag. Been around horses his entire life and the foul stench that erupted the behinds of the animals, made him gag and more often than not forced him to breathe out of his mouth and pinch closed his nostrils. Tonight, he welcomed the pungent odor. Best he could tell, it completely masked the smell of blood, feces and urine coming from the wagon behind him.

How many nights ago had he come out here, informing Elissa that they'd found a body in the woods and thought it might be Alice?

Seemed like yesterday.

It also felt like years ago.

He climbed down from the bench. It might have been dark out, but he saw the prints his boots made as they crunched on fresh snow. He did not see any other tracks.

He could be chasing a false hunch.

He hoped that was the case. Elissa seemed like a nice woman. Grieving the loss of her daughter, she didn't deserve more harassment. Thing was if someone murdered one of his kids, he'd kill them. Plain. Simple. He couldn't admit that openly. He wore a badge. He wasn't above the law. It wouldn't be about legalities, though. It would be all about justice. His justice. If Elissa murdered the Gregory boys, Caleb and Jacob, he'd have to arrest her.

He'd respect her actions, but would still have to bring her in.

The sheriff did a quick once around the place.

The inside of the house was dark. Not a single lantern lit that he could tell.

There was not one footprint in the snow, either.

Place didn't just look quiet, it looked vacant. Unused.

At the front door, O'Sullivan knocked.

The door swung open. Old hinges moaned. Wind whipped snow and leaves into the house. A familiar odor smacked the sheriff's nose. The wallop assaulted his nostrils and they flared. It was the kind of smell that once you've smelt it before, you never forget it. "Ms. Crosby? Hello?"

It was the unmistakable smell of death.

Chapter 33

Jack Raines saw the strobe lights through the front window. He took long strides out of the kitchen and stopped at the bottom of the stairs. Holding onto the rail, he looked up toward the hallway. "Jeremy! Jer!"

Red and blue filled the room. Had to be more than one car out front. This couldn't be a good sign. He touched the screen on his phone. Scrolled through the contacts. He had the lawyer's name and number. The attorney had no idea who he was, though. Calling him this late at night might not be the best idea.

"Jeremy, why don't you come down here?"

Knock. Knock. Knock.

"Jeremy?" Jack sighed and turned around. He opened the front door. "Deputy Schenck. Deputy Mendoza."

They nodded back silent hellos. Mendoza asked, "Where's your nephew, Raines?"

Jack reflexively looked toward the staircase. "I—I'm not sure."

Schenck shouldered his way into the house, made his way up the stairs.

"Hey, you can't do that." Jack looked Mendoza in the eyes. "He can't do that."

She handed him a tri-folded piece of paper. "It's a warrant. We have the authority to search your place. I'm going to ask you to wait outside with Deputy Kelley. He's by the patrol car."

* * *

Jeremy stopped when he saw a hunting shack. Lights were on inside. The ghost had led him here. It was not somewhere he'd been before.

He looked around for the apparition. She was gone. A part of him wanted to call out to her, summon her back. Instead, he remained quiet. Listening for the voice, that didn't come. How could he still have time to save her?

Was Greta inside that house?

Who owned this place?

He should go back and get the sheriff. They would know how to handle this.

They'd want to know how he knew Greta was out here.

They'd want to know how he found the place.

Telling them he'd followed a ghost would get him locked up again.

He wanted to be locked up again.

Not this way, though. Not under some kidnapping suspicion.

He didn't know if Greta was inside or not.

And yet, he knew somewhere inside that shack, he'd find her, but how did he know? How did he find his way here?

He pressed the heels of his hands against the sides of his head. A throbbing started some time ago. It had drummed up to a steady, dull ache.

There is no way he could know Greta was here.

There was no ghost.

Had he taken her? Had he hurt Greta?

He was crying now, bent over with his hands on his knees. His stomach heaved. His vomit splashed onto the snow. Acidic steam rose up from the ground. He backed away, arm out. His hand on a tree steadied him.

He wouldn't accept it, couldn't believe it.

He liked Greta.

She liked him.

There was only one way he could find out, only one way to end the guessing. He had to go inside the shack. He had to see for himself...

* * *

Jack stood with the deputies outside the garage. His hands were stuffed into coat pockets. The officers hadn't found a thing inside the house. While he never thought his nephew was guilty of a thing, he was relieved knowing he'd been right. He hated ever having doubted the boy, even if only for a moment. "Do we get some kind of apology when you don't find anything incriminating?"

Jack knew he shouldn't have said a word. This was the end of their search. They would have been gone in another half hour. He just couldn't bite his tongue. The way Deputy Schenck had rifled through drawers and overturned couch cushions was overkill. The sadistic officer enjoyed himself a little too much.

"Open the garage," Deputy Schenck said. He stood with a hip cocked, his hand resting on the butt of his sidearm.

Jack shook his head but reached down and lifted the garage door. It rolled up, hesitated, as if it might come back down, but stayed in place. Jack took a step back and with a sweep of his arm, invited them in.

Deputies Mendoza and Kelley shined flashlights into the darkness. Schenck found the string dangling from the naked bulb in the center of the garage and gave it a pull.

Jack's smile dropped.

Despite the light, Mendoza shined her flashlight onto the seat of Jeremy's scooter.

"I don't know what that is," Jack said and knew immediately he sounded defensive, guilty even.

"Looks like a pair of women's panties." Mendoza said. He tucked her flashlight under her arm, reached into her coat and removed a folded brown paper bag. Kelley took the bag from her and shook it open.

As Schenck snapped on a pair of latex gloves, Jack said, "Come on. Why would those be right there? Why would anyone leave something like that out in the open for anyone to find? That doesn't even make sense. It's ridiculous."

Schenck lifted the panties and closely examined them before delicately dropping them into the brown bag.

"Where is your nephew, Jack?" Deputy Mendoza's jaw was set. Her eyes were locked on him.

"I don't know."

"Did he go somewhere?"

"He was in the house. We talked. I thought he went up to bed," Jack said.

"Try calling him," she said. "We need to find him. If he knows where Greta is, if that girl is still alive…"

Jack took his cellphone out of his pocket.

He thought he should call the attorney first.

Except, Mendoza was right. It wasn't about Jeremy at the moment. This was about Greta Murray.

Chapter 34

Jeremy made his way closer to the hunting shack. It sat in somewhat of a valley. It was nestled between trees, wood was chopped and stacked under a taut tarp. The front porch had two Adirondack chairs side by side.

Greta couldn't be inside.

The place looked … normal.

The throb inside his head had subsided. The pain was nearly gone.

This was wrong—him out here, pretty much lost in the woods—all wrong.

He should turn around.

If Uncle Jack realized he was missing, he'd be worried. They needed to sit down again and talk.

He was losing his mind.

Had he ever been in control of anything?

Jeremy climbed the two steps up onto the porch. His boots sounded like thunder on the wood. He winced. If anyone was inside, they'd hear him. People in the mountains had rifles and shotguns and preferred shooting first and asking questions later.

He didn't want to get shot.

At the window behind the chairs, Jeremy peeked into the shack.

He saw his mother sprawled out on the kitchen floor, blood pooled around her body. Her eyes were open and looking directly at him. Her mouth moved, but he couldn't hear what she was saying. Was she talking to him?

His father was there, too.

Draped over his mother and crying. "Why couldn't you be faithful? Why couldn't you just stop seeing him?"

Jeremy closed his eyes tight and jumped back, away from the window.

That's what his father had said.

The words hadn't registered, not to an eight year old. Faithful.

He backed into one of the chairs and tumbled over it. He landed on all fours and cringed from a sudden pain sparked behind his kneecap.

The front door opened.

The light from inside the shack cast the figure in the doorway in shadows.

"I don't believe this," the man said and then Jeremy heard the unmistakable sound of a gun cocking.

And at that moment, Jeremy knew the truth.

He understood the past.

His mind filled in the blanks he'd blocked out.

Sheriff Christopher O'Sullivan said, "Get up. Get in here, now."

* * *

Fort Keeps, NY — Adirondacks — October 1912

Elissa Crosby's body hung limp and lifeless from the rafter in her daughter Alice's bedroom. The woman faced the corner and wore a white nightgown. Her skin was blue, her feet and calves were covered in dried mud. On the floor below her was feces and urine. The bowels release when death overtakes a person.

Sheriff Benji O'Sullivan breathed through his mouth and held his lantern up so he could better survey the room.

He figured she'd been dead a day, maybe as long as two days. Dr. Marr would have better insight. He based time of death on when he'd last talked with her. It was before Caleb Gregory was murdered in his cell. He'd meant to come out and check on her, but was more wrapped up in trying to keep the younger brother, Jacob safe.

Suicide was a horrible thing. Although he couldn't find signs of foul play, he couldn't hang his hat on the idea Elissa had taken her own life, just yet.

Somewhere out there, someone had killed two boys.

Part of him had suspected Alice's mother had been responsible. Revenge. It seemed likely. It seemed plausible. It had made her a prime suspect, actually. The sheriff figured it must have been someone close with the Crosby family, if it wasn't Elissa herself.

Now he knew she couldn't have been the one to attack the Gregory boy in the back of the wagon tonight. The hair on the back of his neck stood on end. Not unless she'd found a way to avenge her daughter's death from the other side?

The door behind him slammed closed.

He was alone in the room with the hanging woman.

A cold wind whipped about the room. Impossibly, the flame inside his lantern blew out. He knew something was not right. He didn't dare say the words he thought in his head out loud. He couldn't silence them from screaming inside his mind.

A specter? An apparition?

He dropped the lantern and made a break for the door.

It wouldn't budge.

O'Sullivan heard someone laugh.

A woman.

The only other person in the room was a dangling corpse.

Slowly, O'Sullivan turned around.

Stray light filtered into the room from the window by the bed.

The corpse had turned, faced him.

Elissa's eyes opened. Her hands shot forward. O'Sullivan screamed.

Chapter 35

Jeremy entered the hunting shack. He was shoved from behind. Stumbling forward, he tripped over an ottoman. He went down hard. Again, he struck his knee. Ignoring the pain, he rolled over onto his back and looked up at the sheriff who loomed over him.

The handgun was only a few feet away, but pointed directly at his forehead.

"Jeremy!" Greta was handcuffed to a cast iron hot water radiator. Her hair was matted against her forehead. There was a black blindfold tied over her eyes covering most of her face. Her clothing was torn. Scrapes and bruises covered her arms.

"Are you okay?" he asked.

O'Sullivan kicked Jeremy in the lower thigh. "What are you doing here?"

It wasn't a question.

"I know what you did," Jeremy said. "You killed my father."

"He killed your mother!"

"No, no he didn't. It was an accident," Jeremy said.

"You were eight, what did you know?"

"I didn't know anything then, but I know now. I remember it all now. You came in while they were fighting and you shot my dad," Jeremy said. It all made sense. "You had a hand in having me locked away at St. Mary's all these years."

"Your mother didn't love your father. She loved me. He wasn't going to let her go, though. She told me she was going to leave him, that she was telling him that morning. You're lucky I came by. I knew things wouldn't go well. Your dad was crazy over this—"

"Crazy because he wanted to keep his family together?"

"He killed your mother. He might have killed you, too. I've seen things like that happen. Crimes of passion. Your father wasn't thinking straight. He was out of control."

"You're going to prison for this!"

Sheriff O'Sullivan laughed, but kept his gun trained on Jeremy's head.

There was nothing funny. "Are you okay, Greta?"

"She was okay, kid. She was," O'Sullivan said. "But you've ruined that. You never should have come home. I was going to let her go, you know. *Probably*. Wait a few days, wait until we had you committed back to the hospital and then I'd have let her go. She never knew it was me, that I'd taken her. Not until now, not until this very moment, the minute you showed up. You killed her, Jeremy. Just like you're responsible for the death of your parents."

"I wasn't responsible for their deaths!"

O'Sullivan ran his tongue across his teeth. "Sure you were. Reason your mother couldn't be happy was because of you. She'd have left your father in a heartbeat, a heartbeat, if it weren't for you. You held her down, Jeremy. You held her back."

"That's not true," Jeremy protested.

"And now you've killed Greta, too. There's no way I can let her just leave. Not now. Not when she knows," he waved his gun around, "... all of this. I have to kill her and then I have to kill you. Thing is, I'm still going to make it look like you did it. I'll have everyone believing you went nuts, again, that you went crazy on your little girlfriend here."

Greta struggled against her restraints. The cuffs bit into her flesh.

"Settle down, now, miss. Just settle down," O'Sullivan said.

Jeremy looked around for anything he could use to defend himself against the sheriff. There had to be a way he could attack the man and save Greta. He saw not a single object he could use as a weapon.

"It's not going to be much different than how I framed your father for the death of your mother. Same exact thing. Murder suicide. See 'em all the time. Like I said, crimes of passion. Love, or the illusion of it, is a powerful thing. Maddening for most. Crippling for someone like you. Someone with an already disturbed mind." He laughed. "But you know what, I didn't have you committed. I knew you'd seen me, but I was confident I could convince you you'd seen something completely different that morning. That when I showed up, I tried helping your parents. I'll admit, I was sweating it a little. Worried what you'd say, but then you just stopped talking. You didn't answer any questions. Shock, that's what they thought at first. You were in shock and rightly so. It just, it never went away."

When O'Sullivan shrugged, Jeremy felt anger build inside him. His face felt like it was on fire, his cheeks were so hot.

"Am I making you mad? Huh?" the sheriff pursed his lips. "But then you had to go and come back to Fort Keeps. A few years back when your uncle moved in, I smelled trouble. Then that day when I ran into you, I had to find a way to run into you, I saw it in your eyes. Recognition."

Sheriff O'Sullivan clicked his tongue. "Had to do something, didn't I?"

"Not this," Jeremy said. "You don't have to do this. You can let her go. She isn't going to tell anyone anything. Are you, Greta?"

"Nothing. No. Nothing." Her voice cracked, as if she hadn't spoken in days.

"Well, yeah. I do." O'Sullivan said. "And I'm going to kill her first, Jeremy. I'm going to shoot her in the skull and you're going to watch. I want the weight of this to sink in. She's going to die because of you."

The sheriff raised his gun and aimed it at Greta.

Jeremy was still on his back. All he could do was kick out. His boots caught the sheriff in the shins.

The gun fired.

Greta screamed.

Jeremy rolled onto all fours and twisted around. He sprang toward the sheriff.

The lights inside the shack went out...

Chapter 36

Jeremy collided with the sheriff, drove his shoulder into the man's chest. The two of them crashed onto the floor as the lights inside the shack went out. Jeremy thought they'd landed on a lamp cord, that it might have been yanked out of a plug.

As the Sheriff threw him off, the hairs on the back of Jeremy's neck stood on end.

O'Sullivan knelt over Jeremy and threw punches.

The blows struck Jeremy's body. The wind pushed out of his lungs. He gasped for air.

Another punch slammed into his jaw.

He bit into his tongue and pain raced through his head.

Only when the laughing started, did the beating stop.

O'Sullivan pivoted around on one knee.

Jeremy took advantage of the reprieve and focused on breathing. He heard Greta sobbing by the radiator. If she'd been shot, at least she was still alive.

The sheriff stood. Everything was just shadows. Jeremy couldn't make out much at all. Except he didn't think they were alone.

"No," the sheriff said. "This ... no."

Jeremy looked around the dark room. He saw her, then and he recognized her. She was in the far corner of the room, adjacent to the front window.

He had followed the woman through the woods. She'd led him directly to O'Sullivan's hunting shack and right to Greta.

Pushing up onto his elbows, wincing and wrapping an arm protectively across bruised ribs, Jeremy did his best to sit up.

He looked over at Greta. She was a shadow shackled to a radiator. But she was safe. For now.

Christopher O'Sullivan fired his gun. Once. Twice. Three times.

The woman in the corner unflinchingly remained, unharmed. When the sheriff fired off two more shots, she reacted.

The woman uncoiled like a snake.

She sprang forward, arms out. Taking the sheriff to the ground, like a lion attacking a gazelle, the ghost unrelentingly tore at his flesh with claw-like hands.

The sheriff's body writhed about. He screamed in both pain and terror. His high-pitched cries forced Jeremy to cover his ears. The woman's teeth gnashed on skin and tore at fat. She growled and groaned.

Jeremy thought the ghost was almost in ecstasy as she snapped away ribs and buried her face inside the sheriff's chest cavity.

He wanted to close his eyes and look away, but couldn't.

There was no looking away as the woman sliced through tissue and meat. The sheriff's flailing eventually stopped.

His cries had quit minutes before.

And the woman, resembling more of an animal than anything supernatural, locked her eyes on Jeremy.

She looked feral.

Her illuminated eyes glowed like a cat caught in headlights.

Jeremy pushed his back up against the wall.

The woman stood, covered in blood, she stepped around the dead sheriff, turned and walked into the darkness of the corner.

"Jeremy!" Greta screamed. "Jeremy!"

The ghost turned around. She continued looking at him, eyes glowing. Jeremy could not even blink.

"Jeremy? Someone?"

And then the ghost closed her eyes.

The glow, gone.

The darkness swallowed her.

Greta was crying. "Anyone. Please, someone."

"I'm here, Greta. I'm right here."

The lights came on inside the shack. No plug had fall out from an outlet.

No ghost stood in the corner.

"Jeremy! Jeremy, what happened? What's going on?"

Her blindfold was a blessing. The sheriff was shredded. Blood was everywhere. Jeremy snatched a key ring off the corpse and stepped around the mess, his stomach turning over and twisting around inside his gut.

"You're safe," Jeremy said and unfastened the cuffs.

Greta went to lift away the blindfold.

"Don't," he warned. "Just, please, just keep it on."

Chapter 37

Dr. Marr confirmed Elissa Crosby died before the first Gregory boy died in his jail cell. That cleared her name, but Sheriff Benji O'Sullivan wasn't sure if it cleared her soul. He never told anyone about what happened in Alice's bedroom the night he found Elissa dangling from a noose. A mind tends to play tricks when in haunting situations. He'd let himself get spooked was all. There was no way her blue corpse spun around on the end of the rope and reached for him. No way at all.

Elissa Crosby didn't have much except for the patch of land her small house was built on. Most people didn't. Times were tough.

The sheriff had both Elissa and her daughter, Alice's, remains cremated.

Best place in the Adirondacks was where he had built a small hunting cabin deep in the woods. It was tranquil up there. His getaway from everything.

He took their ashes up to the cabin with him that weekend. He ate a satisfying venison dinner and then opened the Good Book to Corinthians and read: "So will it be with the resurrection of the dead. The body that is sown is perishable, it is raised imperishable; it is sown in dishonor, it is raised in glory; it is sown in weakness, it is raised in power; it is sown a natural body, it is raised a spiritual body. If there is a natural body, there is also a spiritual body."

He closed the Bible and set it down on the kitchen table.

Dr. Marr had placed the ashes together into a small tin box. O'Sullivan stepped outside with the box. The wind was whiny and moaned, as if impatient about the gift he was about to offer up. The sheriff breathed in a deep breath and removed the lid. As he exhaled, he shook the ashes out of the box. And the wind accepted the ashes greedily.

O'Sullivan stayed on the front porch a moment longer, waiting, listening, not knowing what he thought might happen.

When nothing happened, he sighed and went back inside.

It was rare when he read more than a verse or two from the Bible in one night. With so few words used, each verse contained so much that deserved contemplation.

This was a night for contemplation, but also a night for comfort. The kind of comfort he sought only came from God.

He sat at the kitchen table and ran his hands over the leather binding before lifting it in his hands and randomly opening to a page.

The rumors started. Whispers riddled townsfolk. Revenge had been taken for the untimely and brutal death of a young girl. People claimed they saw someone, something, wander through the trees. Young boys claimed they heard a woman's voice carried by the wind. When pressed for details they all said the same thing. The presence wanted to know where her daughter was.

Did the Adirondacks now have a vengeful ghost in the woods looking to punish boys for hurting girls?

It was a ludicrous thought, but one he could not easily dismiss.

* * *

Fort Keeps - 6 Months Later

Jeremy stood outside the house, his hands stuffed into his pockets and waited while Uncle Jack finished paperwork with the realtor. The For Sale sign was at the end of the driveway, by the road. Their belongings were packed tight in the back of the truck. Movers were coming by later for the boxed items still inside.

"Weren't planning on leaving without saying goodbye, were you?" Greta sauntered up the driveway. She was dressed as it were still five below zero, hands inside gloves, head under a wool hat and snug in a heavy winter jacket.

"Wouldn't think of it."

She looked at the truck and back at him. "I don't believe you."

He didn't believe himself, either. He didn't understand the pain goodbyes caused, until he thought about leaving Fort Keeps. Then he felt it.

Greta had stood by him during the entire investigation. Police wanted him tried for the death of Sheriff Christopher O'Sullivan.

They had a body, but no proof Jeremy had been responsible. The weapon used for slicing up the sheriff was never found.

Jeremy had told investigators, "I found Greta locked to a radiator inside the shack. The sheriff was there and threatened to kill us both."

"And what happened?" Deputy Mendoza had asked.

"He let us go." It was a simple lie. Greta agreed to it. Everything else, they planned on telling the truth. By saying he'd let them go, Jeremy wouldn't have to explain what really happened to the sheriff. He wouldn't have to mention anything about ghosts, about Elissa Crosby still roaming the woods, still protecting innocent young girls.

"After he admitting killing your father?"

"He said we could leave."

"So why did he take Greta, why did he kidnap your girlfriend?"

"Because, he wanted me locked away."

"Why?"

"I don't know, I guess because he was afraid I would tell someone he'd killed my father."

"You know that doesn't make sense."

"What doesn't?"

"If Christopher didn't want to be arrested for allegedly murdering your father and then for supposedly kidnapping your girlfriend, he wouldn't have let either of you go, now would he?" Mendoza's eyes bore into him. She didn't blink.

Jeremy shrugged. "But he did. He just let us go."

"And you didn't see what happened to him?"

"I heard about it. Later…"

The prosecution's case against Jeremy fell apart as fast as they threw one together. During depositions Greta Murray explained that she'd been abducted on her walk home. Someone had attacked her from behind. When she woke up, her pants and underwear were missing. She was handcuffed to a radiator and blindfolded.

Her abductor never said a word, until Jeremy showed up that night.

The two argued and she did her best sharing with the attorneys present everything Jeremy and Sheriff O'Sullivan said.

"But how did you know it was Sheriff O'Sullivan if you were blindfolded?"

"I recognized his voice."

"How can you be sure it was Sheriff O'Sullivan and not someone else?"

"When I was dating his son, I ate dinner with the sheriff nearly three nights a week. I knew the sheriff's voice quite well."

"And you heard the sheriff say he was going to let you go?"

"Not at first."

"What did he say first?"

"That he was going to kill me and make Jeremy watch and then he was going to kill Jeremy."

"You heard the man who had abducted you say this?"

"Sheriff O'Sullivan, yes. I heard him say that."

* * *

"I've got something for you," Jeremy said.

"For me?" Greta smiled.

He walked over to the garage and opened the door.

There was a piece of paper taped on the seat of his scooter. "I want you to have my scooter."

She looked at the message on the paper. On it was her name and address. "You were going to leave without saying goodbye, weren't you?"

"I don't know."

She lowered her head and whispered, "We never talked about what happened that night."

"We never should, either." Jeremy hadn't had any issues sleeping in the house, in his room, since the night Elissa saved them. The ghost had led him through the woods. He'd been able to find Greta, but Elissa, she was the hero, the one protecting innocent girls from wicked men. "I'm going to miss you, you know."

"You're only going down to Rochester. I'm sure we'll see each other still." She smiled, again.

Seeing each other sounded good.

It would never happen.

Life would interfere.

"I'm counting on it."

"I can take this here scooter of mine and drive all the way to Rochester any time I want now." She laughed, but then the smile faded. She stood on her toes and hugged him, wrapping her arms around his neck. Pulling him close, she whispered in his ear, "You better text me all the time."

* * *

With grey hair at the temples and dressed in a sport coat, dress shirt and silk tie, Jeremy Raines sat alone at the table in the center of the restaurant. He did his best ignoring the couple across from him. They'd forgotten about their meals and had reverted to blatantly staring at him.

When they stood up, he knew there was no escaping them.

"We're so sorry," the man said.

"We hate to bother you and all," the woman said.

"But, you're him, aren't you?" the man said.

Jeremy tried smiling. He hoped it didn't come off as a grimace. "Ah, yeah."

The couple looked at each other and almost squealed with delight. "Knew it. I knew it," the man said. "We have all of your books."

"All of them," the woman verified. "We've got to be your biggest fans. And when we buy your book—"

"We buy two." The man held up two fingers, perfectly illustrating two. "Want to know why?"

"We can't wait for the other to finish reading the book first," the woman said.

"We read them at the same time!"

"I appreciate that. I really do."

"We don't have any copies with us, but maybe you could sign a napkin or something for us?"

"My pleasure." He scrawled out a signature. Thought about it and signed a second napkin.

"Is it too much to ask for a picture?" They flagged down a waiter. Handed off their phone. And then crawled into his personal space smiling for the flash. "Thank you, thank you so much!"

He couldn't be upset with them. When he started writing books he never expected wealth, or fame. The books took off. *Woman in the Woods* shot to number one on the New York Times Bestseller List. Every book after did the same. "It was my pleasure."

He watched them, watch him, as they made their way back to their table.

"Am I interrupting?"

Jeremy got to his feet. "Greta! When did you get here?"

"Oh, about the time they started walking up to you."

"You could have saved me from them, you know," he said, pulling out the chair across from him. She sat down.

"What? And miss watching you squirm? Never." She reached for his hand across the table. "I'm sorry I'm late. I just wanted to make sure the kids were all set."

"Uncle Jack's got everything under control. We get one date night out a month, and you," he looked at his wrist, where there was no watch, "are five minutes late, young lady."

She giggled. "Anticipation, old man. Anticipation."

THE END

About the Author

Phillip Tomasso is an award-winning, Amazon Best Selling author of more than twenty-six novels. He works full-time as a Fire / EMS Dispatcher for 911. Aside from writing, and time spent with family, Tomasso enjoys playing guitar, and singing. However, to hear him sing you might disagree. As always, Tomasso is at work on his next novel. Please be sure to visit his website, follow him on Twitter, and Like his Author Page on Facebook. You can also email Tomasso with any reviews, comments, or requests for Guest Speaking at: phillip@philliptomasso.com

http://www.philliptomasso.com/
www.twitter.com/P_Tomasso
www.facebook.com/authorphilliptomasso

Special Thanks

I want to give special thanks to my Beta Readers. They are heroes in my book (pun intended). Morgan "Ms. Morgs" Gleisle, Katie "K-Pop" Popielarz, Susan Bates, Roseann Powell, Corrine Chorney, and last but certainly not least, Alyson Read. These ladies , on numerous occasions, helped flesh out the ideas for this novella, read countless drafts, provided feedback, aided in direction and were patient with my constant babble while writing the story. Additionally, I would like to thank my publisher Miika Hannila and the team at Creativia Publishing. They continue to see value in my tales, and for that—for them—I am grateful.

Printed by Amazon Italia Logistica S.r.l.
Torrazza Piemonte (TO), Italy

13069625R00107